KIT
and
KITTY

by Sarah Carlisle

FAWCETT COVENTRY • NEW YORK

KIT AND KITTY

Published by Fawcett Coventry Books, a unit of CBS Publications, the Consumer Publishing Division of CBS Inc.

ISBN: 0-449-50202-3

Printed in the United States of America

First Fawcett Coventry printing: August 1981

10 9 8 7 6 5 4 3 2 1

One

"Dash it all, Lady Madge, what am I to do?" Kit de Fleming asked for the sixth time. His look of anguish amused his hostess, a woman of mature charms that were skillfully enhanced with the aid of cosmetics and her dressmaker.

"Darling Kit, do come and sit by me. It can't be all as shockingly dreary as you say! Come, dearest." She managed to lure him away from his dramatic stance in the bow window of her boudoir. A sensible woman, she avoided the strong light of day that was streaming through the sparkling glass panes.

"There! That is much more comfortable. Now we can discuss the whole thing calmly," she murmured soothingly. "There is really no need for your distress. We are two sensible people who shall deal with this problem in a sensible manner!"

"Sensible? How can one be sensible in the face of such wanton, unfeeling cruelty?" he protested vehemently. "The whole notion that I should marry a mere chit of a girl, a mere schoolroom miss whom I have never seen, is preposterous!"

"Now, darling, you are a man of the world and there are certain worldly aspects to the match which make it a very practical one indeed." She gently caressed his cheek with one long, white finger, then looked up at him with supplication clear in her eyes. He really was a most attractive youth, but so headstrong! "You do see that, don't you? It will solve so many problems."

"I suppose you refer to the money she will one day inherit?" he asked with disdain, glaring down his long, straight nose at some distant part of her carpet. "I have no patience with such sordid considerations!"

Lady Madge, who did, bit her lip but gave no further sign of her exasperation. "Kit, you know that your uncle's title, when you come into it, is at best an empty honor. His estates have long since been mortgaged for the last few pounds he could get to cover his gambling debts. When this other brother of his dies, you will be saddled with debt and responsibility. You will not be able to rely forever on your mother's generosity, which would not put things to rights in any case. Nor will your inheritance from your father suffice. You need a large amount of capital, an amount as large as what this girl will inherit."

"I don't care about the title," he said indignantly, throwing back from his brow a stray lock of hair. "The new Lord Helm, my inestimable Uncle

Matthew, is said to be warm in the pockets. Let him see to it."

"You do yourself proud with your sentiments regarding the title, but it will one day be yours, nonetheless, along with the responsibilities it carries! As to relying on your uncle, well, you know as well as I how things have stood all these years between him and your mother. There is no hope there! Miss Leyburne's fortune would go far toward putting to rights the shocking affairs of your family's estates."

It would also do rather well for her own untidy collection of bills hidden away in her closed escritoire, but there would be time for that later.

"I never asked for such a burden to be placed on my shoulders!" he protested.

"Of course not. But it will fall there nonetheless. You will have in your care the welfare of *many* people who have served your family for *many* years!"

"The money isn't even hers yet," he grumbled.

"But it will be, darling. She will get a sizable dowry on marriage, and Mrs. Brampton has made no secret of her plans to bequeath the whole of her fortune on her godchild. Everyone knows just how large a fortune it is. Mr. Brampton is most successful."

"It smells of trade! Brampton is a mere cit. Would you have me make an alliance with a mushroom?"

"Miss Leyburne's connections are quite impeccable," Lady Madge said absently, noticing with some concern that one of her fingernails had somehow managed to split. Kit's abrupt rise to his feet drew her attention back to him with a start. Her argument, so well thought out and repeated with boring frequency, had nearly lulled her into inattentiveness. She brought all her powers to bear on this troublesome young man before her. She never doubted her ability to sway him.

"Think of the charming old couple you told me of, the headgroom and his wife. Dear me, my memory is so dreadful, I can never recall names, but I believe you called him Joshua Checkers. He taught you to ride when you were a boy."

"You remember that!" He was at her side in a moment, a look of pleased admiration on his face. "Lady Madge, that you should bother to recall something I had said in passing, the merest trifle! I am overwhelmed!"

"Dearest Kit!" she said affectionately. "I bother with everything *you* tell me."

"You are too good to me!" he protested.

The lady, her mind dwelling ironically on the expensive trinkets and bits of jewelry he had showered on her, as well as the small loans of cash, murmured with a great show of sincerity, "On the contrary, Kit, you are too good to me."

There was a long moment of silence while he pressed her hand to his lips. She allowed him some gentle kisses on her fingers and then said, "It is this very goodness which must impel you to accept your mother's suggestion. No, no, don't pull away from me so! You make a painful duty even more difficult for me."

"I can never love anyone but you, dearest, dearest Madge. Never!" he whispered starkly.

Lady Madge hid her doubts with a brave smile.

"And I, too, will never know another love like ours!" she answered, her voice lowering dramatically.

"Then how can you tell me to wed another?"

"We are creatures of the world and must face our responsibilities, darling. Society places certain demands on us, sometimes unbearable ones, that we cannot ignore."

"We shall flee together! I shall carry you off to the Continent. Your husband would never pursue us there!"

Lady Madge knew that she need flee no further than Kensington and her lord would still not bother to pursue. Although still living together under the same roof, they had long since gone their separate ways, each indifferent to the actions of the other. It was this last fact she had left Kit unaware of. A jealous husband was an excellent excuse when other matters, including a rich, elderly admirer, claimed her attention.

"It would mean dishonor!" she gasped with horror.

"But for love, my darling! For the great love we share! That makes everything right," he argued urgently.

"And the Checkers and others like them? What of that? Can you turn your back on your heritage? If you can tell me yes to that question, you cannot be the same young man I thought you were! The young man I fell in love with!" She had removed a lace handkerchief from the bosom of her dress and was delicately dabbing at her eyes, her shoulders turned away from Kit in her distress.

"My darling love, don't say that to me!"

"To propose such a course of action would only destroy the love I feel for you," she whispered, her voice muffled by the lace. "Do not press it on me!"

"No, no, you mustn't say that!"

"I will never be able to see you, ever again!"

"I can't live without you!" Kit looked desperately at her resolute back. He held out his hand to touch it, then drew back. What was he to do? "You ask too much of me," he said, his voice low and breaking with anguish.

"You must promise never to mention an elopement with me. Never breathe a word of it! Don't even think of it!"

"For your love I will do what I must. Anything you wish of me, you have only to ask. Anything!"

Lady Madge let escape a sigh of relief, well hidden by the lace. Glancing shyly over her shoulder, her face still screened by the handkerchief, she asked, "Anything?"

Kit had sunk to his knees before her, seeking to capture one of her hands. "Anything."

Sniffing and dabbing her eyes, the lady smiled at him bravely. "I do so want to be proud of you! If I were the cause of your dishonor, I would want to die. Truly I would!"

"Never that," Kit said gently. "You are so lovely now. You are the most beautiful woman in the world! Please forgive me for causing you to cry, but your tears have made your eyes sparkle like stars in a midnight sky! So many women are unattractive when they weep, but you are a goddess, The Goddess of Tragedy!"

Smiling at these fulsome compliments, Lady Madge tucked her entirely dry handkerchief back into the bosom of her dress and turned to face Kit, her cheek offered for a chaste kiss. He really was a dear boy, and so handsome! She could ride in the Park with him in his carriage and feel nothing but pride that she had such a handsome escort. Pity he was still two years short of his majority and unable to control his fortune. Even more of a pity that the fortune was such a small one.

"Then it is agreed! We shall not mention this dreadful business ever again. Between two such friends, it will be as if your marriage never existed!" she said bracingly.

"It is still a distasteful matter," Kit said sadly. "And I greatly fear that such a loveless match will be unfair to Miss Leyburne. She has every right to expect more."

"Unfair?" Lady Madge lifted her elegantly clad shoulders disdainfully. "It is done every day. Young ladies in her position expect such things and accept them!"

Kit looked at her intently, a faint shadow of unease crossing his face. "Still . . ."

She laughed away his scruples. "Darling boy, she will become a countess some day, which is very fair indeed! And you will acquire her fortune and set to rights your estates. These are facts of life that are understood on both sides. And I know that you will be very kind to her, far more kind than many other men would be," she ended, adding a caressing note to her voice.

"I shall certainly do my duty," he said in a dull voice. Then a laugh escaped his lips. "I shan't even be able to touch her fortune when we are married! It will be some time before there will be any question of receiving it. Mrs. Brampton is in the heartiest of health!"

"Perhaps you can claim some small part of the money immediately," his love said casually. "Or borrow on your expectations." Seeing the look of distaste on his face, she hurried to add, "To benefit in any way you can deserving people such as the Deckers. You might write that into the marriage contract, about an advance, you know. No one would question it."

"Checkers."

"What?" She stared at him with blank incomprehension for a moment, then caught his meaning. "Yes, Checkers! How foolish of me. That was what I meant to say," she agreed with a brilliant smile, covering her slip with her usual charm. "You are such an adorable man, dearest Kit! How have I deserved such good fortune to have captured your heart? In all other things my luck has failed dismally!" And with a mind toward some of the more pressing of her creditors, she began a winsome tale of a card party, merely a small, private affair, where she had lost the paltry sum of one hundred pounds.

Two

He was the handsomest man in the whole world, of that she was certain. The tallest, the strongest, the kindest, handsomest man in the world. And he had bowed to her from the back of his very tall, black horse, actually sweeping off his hat to her! She could not believe her good fortune that he had even noticed her, much less deigned to acknowledge her presence in such a grand way.

She and Carter, her maid who had served her since she was a very small girl, always walked in the Park at precisely the same hour of the afternoon. It was a very sedate walk, along the Park Lane to the entrance that Mama insisted they use, down a certain path that wound its way past flower beds, to the lake where they sat on the bench. Or rather, Carter sat on the rustic wooden seat and Kitty fed the ducks with bread she had begged from Cook. Then back along the same route until they had reached the door of her parents' very respectable London residence, to be greeted by the footman on duty. All far different from her rambles on the fells.

It was a pleasant enough walk, particularly if the weather was fine, which wasn't often, and Mama and Mrs. Brampton said the fresh air would do her good. Sometimes they saw other young ladies, with their maids, on similar expeditions. Mama was very strict about whom she was to speak with in the Park; only the daughters and granddaughters and nieces of the families her parents associated with were to be engaged in conversation. There were days when this made for a very dull outing indeed. No one acceptable would be about, except the ducks, and she wasn't even sure that Mama would approve of her feeding them, for she had avoided mentioning it. It could even be dull on the days when there were acquaintances to meet, for the young ladies her mother encouraged her to be friendly with were very proper and well-mannered but never seemed to have anything to say. They came from the most conservative Tory families in the realm, for her mother had a horror of anything that smacked of Whiggery, and Kitty had concluded that they were one and all taught as little as possible in the hopes that this training would enable them never to think of anything new and different. If in fact these other young ladies were capable of thinking at all.

She had said something of this, not to Mama, but to Papa, and he had said that he rather thought that once she had been presented to society she would find all this very different. And then he had turned the conversation with a smile and a kiss and they never again referred to it.

On the whole, she preferred the ducks.

When the handsome man first appeared along the route she took, it was only natural that she would take notice of him. He added a spice of adventure to her walks, being the only thing of interest she encountered, on the whole. He was always on horseback, an odd fact in itself, because her path was far from the fashionable trails of the Ton. He had simply appeared one afternoon, intent on handling his fresh mount, shying along the bridle path near the lake. She had immediately found him attractive, there was nothing even remotely as compelling as he in the vicinity, and she had fallen desperately in love. In his elaborate uniform, mounted on a spirited horse, he was the stuff of her dreams.

He had curly blond hair that tumbled down a high, noble forehead and into sideburns along gaunt, hollow cheeks, to meet in a thick, military moustache that covered his upper lip. His eyes were a piercing blue, set deeply beneath fine brows, his nose strong and purposeful. She could not see as much of his mouth as she would have liked, for the moustache covered it slightly with its droop, but his chin had an interesting cleft that softened its squareness. His carriage in the saddle was impeccable, always erect and commanding, his boots immaculately polished, and his uniform superb!

She had no knowledge of regiments and medals

and such things. All she saw was a vision in scarlet, with elaborate facings and straps and sashings, sparkling with the reflections from ribbons and clasps and gold braid. His coat fit him to perfection and his linen, such that showed, was always snowy white. His shako sat firmly on his head, never wavering despite the motion of his mount, but the plume that soared above it reflected the slightest of breezes and his every movement. He was everything she had always thought a soldier should be.

She wondered if he had been wounded in some distant battle. He looked pitifully thin in the face, although his shoulders were broad and strong and his figure becomingly full. In fact, he was what Mama and her friends would call a fine figure of a man.

But the face!

She studied every line and hollow in it covertly as the days slipped by. Some mornings there were extra shadows under the eyes, deeper creases between nose and mouth. She was sure that he suffered greatly, perhaps spending sleepless nights in the thrall of the pain from a wound gained in battle. She wished she could help him, nurse him tenderly, offer him what comfort she could, for she was sure that he needed precisely that—the care of a gentle, loving woman. In her daydreams she never doubted that she was capable of doing this superbly well. One morning, when he looked particularly haggard, she even dared to ask Carter about the gentleman's drawn face, her concern was so great. She hoped that the opinion of the older, more experienced woman would reassure her, her knowledge inform her. Carter, a sensible country woman, had sniffed contemptuously and put it down to the obvious reason.

"Too much carousing, Miss Kitty."

"Carousing?" Kitty was shocked.

"Just that. Late nights, revelries, and too much drink and gambling for high stakes and . . ." The maid stopped herself. It would never do to say just what else had contributed to the officer's weariness, not to Miss Kitty. She was an innocent, sheltered little thing, as was proper to her station in life.

"Surely not, Carter!"

"Suit yourself, miss!" Carter already regretted her too ready tongue. The miss's feelings had been disturbed, she could tell.

Kitty had struggled for several days with this picture of her gallant. She had loved and trusted Carter all her life, and recognized that there were some things of which the older woman had far greater knowledge than she, a mere chit of a girl of genteel upbringing, would ever expect to encounter. Carter had always been reliable in the past, even to the point of not telling Mama of certain of her activities that parent would have disapproved of. Could the maid be correct in her interpretations of the officer's state of health? Could he really have behaved in such a manner? How could she reconcile this with her own feelings?

With her inexperience, Kitty grew to accept the fact that there was one set of conduct for the gentlemen, particularly military ones, and quite another for the ladies. She had always known that, but in an abstract, impersonal way, her life being muffled all about with the company of women. She had had little to do with men, and certainly not young gentlemen, and she shouldn't be shocked if the handsome officer adhered to a mode of life that society on the whole tolerated and even encouraged. Who knew what sorry experience had driven him to seek solace in drinking and gambling? She was sure that the love of a good woman, a truly sympathetic lady who would give him something better to live for, would be the making of him.

Carter's scorn had only made him seem all the more attractive to young Kitty.

And so she spun out her fantasies about the soldier. He had been wounded rescuing a comrade from the enemy's fire. He had been captured while carrying out some mission of valor that had put him behind the enemy line, jeopardizing his life, and they had imprisoned him and caused him to endure unimaginable hardships. She saw him stepping forward to volunteer for some impossible task while all others hung back in the face of such grave dangers. These very dangers were what caused him to want to go, he was a man of incredible courage and honor who must meet every challenge. He had no will to live, in any case, for his childhood sweetheart had died of a fever while he was away on campaign and his heart had been turned to stone. . . .

These were all very happy and satisfying fantasies. She saw him in battle, sword drawn, leading a charge, or in a rough camp caring for a wounded companion. It was the stuff of her innocence, but she would never have dreamed of sharing it with anyone else. She had no friends her own age to confide in, Mama would never approve, Papa was rarely about, and Carter, who was the closest thing to filling the roll for her of confidant, would never understand.

In this last she did her loyal maid an injustice. Carter did understand and indulge the young miss's whims. She cheerfully lingered by the lake when it was well past the time they were expected home, she would willingly allow her charge to roam a bit farther down a path the gentleman had taken, farther than Mrs. Leyburne would have approved, and after her one excursion into bluntness, she had maintained a discrete silence on the subject of the interesting gentleman. Above all, she had not told her young lady's mother what made these afternoon walks, previously so tedious, now attractive. She had the wisdom to recognize the need for such daydreams, for they were an important part of the life of a young girl who was allowed few companions her own age and no activities that provided an outlet for a lively imagination and curiosity. She knew that once Miss Kitty was properly married, all this would be left behind. And if there was any truth in what Lucas, Mrs. Leyburne's personal maid, had said, that would be soon enough.

Kitty, floating along the pavement, unaware of her surroundings or even of the fact that she was walking along the street to her home and no longer treading the paths of the Park, was treasuring her one and only moment of contact, however brief, with the handsome man. Into it she was investing all the meaning she so desperately lacked in her own life, the warmth that was sadly missing in so much of her existence, and the hope for a happy future with the husband she loved. It was only due to Carter's careful guiding hand that she avoided an abrupt encounter with two pedestrians and a horse.

When they entered the door of the Leyburne townhouse, they were greeted by Jameson, the butler, an unusual mark of distinction.

"Miss Katherine, I trust that you had a pleasant walk in the Park," he said as he watched Carter deftly remove the young lady's bonnet and pelisse.

"Oh, yes, Jameson, it was lovely!"

"Indeed?" The weather was in fact quite chilly and there was the promise of rain in the air, but it was not the butler's duty to question the young miss's statements.

"Mrs. Leyburne and Mrs. Brampton are in the Yellow Salon. Mrs. Leyburne has requested that you join them there."

"Oh." This was not good news for Kitty. When her mother summoned her to attend her straight from a walk, it usually boded a scolding for the girl. Mrs. Brampton's presence was even more ominous, for she was a high stickler, despite her husband's association with trade, and had the most vaunting ambitions for her goddaughter, ambitions that seemed to require an astonishing degree of attention to the niceties of conduct from Kitty. Kitty privately thought that it was Mrs. Brampton who urged her mother into an attitude of unrelenting strictness, for she was not so in the country. It promised to be an uncomfortable interview for her, and she hadn't the least idea of what she had done wrong.

"You'd best run along to your mother, Miss Kitty. I'll just take your things upstairs to your room," Carter said, attempting to brace the child's courage with a hearty, matter-of-fact tone.

"Yes, I must go immediately. Oh, is my hair quite tidy? And my dress? It would never do to have Mrs. Brampton and Mama see me in a state that is anything less."

Carter, who agreed with the shrewdness of this comment, although she disliked the necessity of it, inspected Kitty's hair and dress and nodded her approval. "There's not a curl out of place, not a tear or speck of dirt. You're looking pretty as a picture."

"Thank you." In her nervousness, Kitty appeared not to hear the compliment she had received, only the tone of encouragement, despite the rarity of flattery in her life. She was looking forward with considerable trepidation to what lay ahead. Following Jameson down the hall, she was soon ushered into her mother's presence.

"Katherine, darling, do come here and sit next to your godmama," Mrs. Brampton requested cordially.

Kitty, shocked and relieved with this reception, obeyed willingly, and after a curtsey to her mother and her guest, sat on the love seat.

"Katherine, dear, we have the greatest piece of good news for you," Mrs. Leyburne began as soon as the butler had withdrawn.

"Yes, Mama?"

The good lady ignored the note of caution in her

daughter's voice and continued with every sign of enthusiasm. "We have found a match for you! Quite a brilliant one!"

"A match?" Fear knifed through her.

"Yes. With young Christopher de Fleming. He is the heir of the Earl of Helm, you know, he's the old count's great-grandson. Isn't that the most exciting thing imaginable?"

"But I have never met him!" Kitty said in a voice so faint that neither of the ladies took it for a protest. "Besides, I mean, he can't possibly wish to marry me."

"You will meet him soon enough. He and his mama are to call on us tomorrow afternoon, so that we can all meet and become better acquainted. Perhaps a walk in the Park would be a suitable setting for such a romantic moment," Mrs. Brampton sighed. "You will soon be married, my dear, and we must now begin to think of you as a woman. A few moments alone with the young man will be quite in order."

"In the Park?" Kitty was horrified.

"You needn't worry, my dear, Carter will be there, of course, following you at a discreet distance," her mother assured her, misinterpreting the girl's reaction, and quite pleased with it. "We would never ask you to do something so improper as to walk about unchaperoned in the company of a gentleman. Never fear." She smiled at Kitty, on the whole pleased with the girl's conduct in the face of such awesome news. Katherine was displaying a restraint and feminine delicacy that was all together attractive and becoming.

Kitty was too upset to speak. What could she

do? An overwhelming desire to cry was upon her, but she could not do it here, in the salon, in the presence of her mother and Mrs. Brampton. Particularly Mrs. Brampton, who looked like a well-fed cat at the moment, very pleased with herself and her plans. She would have to find the solace of tears in the privacy of her own bedroom, away from the eyes of all but those of the ever faithful Carter.

Mrs. Brampton, seeing her agitation, sought to rally her. "I know you have been promised a Season, but he is really quite a handsome lad. You are very lucky! This is all really for the best, for when you meet the Ton, it will be as a distinguished married lady. Your mama and I have arranged for you to have not only an eligible husband, but one who is most attractive and courteous and very kind. And you are of the same age, my dear. That will be ever so much more comfortable for you than to be married to an older man, which is the fate of so many young girls who are unfortunate enough to have careless, indifferent parents or guardians. Your mama and I have taken every care for your future happiness!"

"And you will be very, very happy, my dear," her mother added. "I am sure that the two of you will fall in love when you but lay eyes on one another." And she was sincere in what she said. The combination of Mrs. Brampton's arguments and her own wishful thinking had convinced her it was to be.

"And just think! You will be a countess some day! The mistress of a London townhouse and no fewer than three country residences," Mrs. Brampton murmured, enraptured with the vision of greatness before her. "A great hostess! A leading peeress of the realm!"

With Kitty sitting there in dumb misery, the two ladies nodded their satisfaction. Imagine! A young and handsome husband who would one day inherit a title.

Wealth, position, independence—what more could a young girl ask for?

Three

Kitty cried herself to sleep that night. She had had to hold back the tears for many hours, through a long and tedious afternoon and an even longer evening. Dinner was nearly more than she could endure; her mother and Mrs. Brampton could not leave the subject of her betrothal alone. Her father was absent, so there was no respite from that quarter. It was perhaps fortunate for Kitty that the two ladies were so full of enthusiastic talk, for otherwise they would have noticed her own silence and commented on it unfavorably. A young lady of breeding was expected to maintain gracious conversation at table.

She didn't want to get up the next morning. Vague thoughts of claiming illness flitted through her distressed imagination. Perhaps she could fall into a decline and waste away to nothing. That would be far preferable to this proposed marriage. At the root of her distress was her love for the officer, a very real and strong emotion for all its fantastical nature. She had reached the peak of her feelings for him with that simple bow of the afternoon before. Her secret affection distorted her perception of the fate planned for her, more so than it would have at any other time. She had always assumed that she would marry for love, not convenience; she had always guessed her parents had done so. And now, in her heart she was convinced that she was being thwarted in true love, torn from her commitment to a man whom she wholly loved.

It was Carter who insisted that she leave her bed at the usual hour of the morning.

"Now, miss, you must have some breakfast."

"I don't want any. I'm not hungry." Kitty tried to hide her head beneath her down-filled coverlet, to no avail. Carter pulled it off with firm, relentless hands and stood towering over her. On this morning, the usually motherly maid seemed a scourging fury to her hapless mistress.

"Now, now, that won't do. You must eat something. And you know that your mother will be distressed if you don't appear at the breakfast table. She'll be inquiring after you, worrying that you're ill or something."

"I don't care! Tell her I am ill. I am sure that I have a fever, Carter."

Carter obligingly held a hand to the girl's forehead. "No, I don't think so. And if you *are* ill, that means that she'll come herself to see what is wrong. You know that."

It was an unscrupulous tactic, but it worked. Of late, Kitty had a horror of her mother entering her rooms, for these were her refuge from the difficulties of the daily life she led. Carter was right. At the first sign of sickness, Mrs. Leyburne would assume the role of tender nurse, and invade the sickroom with at least one doctor in attendance. Under no circumstances would Kitty allow this to happen.

"Oh, very well," she grumbled. She slid out of her bed and padded barefoot over to her dressing table. Carter brought out a simple morning dress from the wardrobe, laid it on the table, then raised Kitty's hands over her head. In a few minutes the night shift was pulled off and laid in its drawer, the dress and its accessories buttoned into place; Kitty was turned around to sit before the mirror to have her hair brushed and arranged in the simple style her mother approved of. Kitty, usually docile, was now totally indifferent to what was being done for her.

Carter brushed her hair for longer than usual, drawing the boar's bristles through the thick, light brown hair with studied calm. It was a very soothing rhythm, maintained from long practice, and after a few minutes she could feel Miss Kitty relaxing slightly. She looked at the girl in the mirror, fondly remembering her in her childhood, a mere bit of a thing with pleasing manners and a loving nature. Now the maid saw a young lady in the first bloom of her beauty. Her affectionate eyes recognized that in a year or two, Kitty would be a diamond of the first order. The delicate brow and nose, wide-spaced brown eyes, the soft, wide mouth with its hint of sensuality combined with her developing figure, would turn the head of any young man. Her complexion was unusually clear and vibrant, bringing out the molding of her face for attention and underscoring a beauty that even old age would fail to mar. It was a pity that this marriage would happen so soon. In a year or two Kitty would have had her choice of eager, romantic suitors, rather than the coldness of an arranged marriage. Then she shrugged her shoulders. Who was she to question the ways of her betters? Only the other day she had been thinking that what the miss needed was a husband, and Mrs. Leyburne and Mrs. Brampton had arranged for just that, although what the master would say was anybody's guess. She hoped that it would be a happy marriage, reminding herself that many such couples managed quite well.

As for Kitty, only her careful training enabled her to move through the morning's activities with composure. A leisurely breakfast, with only herself and her mother present, an hour spent with her French studies, and another for music, the time until lunch filled with needlework under her mother's guidance, then another meal that went by all too quickly. Kitty prayed for sickness, an accident, disaster, a miracle. None was forthcoming.

She and Mrs. Leyburne were in the Yellow Salon when the Honorable Mrs. Bernard de Fleming and Mr. Christopher de Fleming were announced. Jameson ushered the honored guests into the room, using even more dignity for them than Kitty would have thought humanly possible. The whole household knew of the importance of the visit and each member in his or her own way sought to contribute to the success of the event. Jameson's attitude reflected the solemnity of the occasion. A Great Match was being made, and all hoped for Miss Kitty's happiness.

It wanted only the arrival of Mrs. Brampton to start the business at hand, and that lady arrived with the bustle of importance one finds in those who meddle in the affairs of others.

At first Kitty could only bring herself to look at the floor near the newcomers' feet. Then she steeled herself to speak to Mrs. de Fleming as was proper. She desperately focused all her attention on the lady, and found herself bemused by a replica of her mother: short, square, but with a determined chin that quite belied the broad, friendly smile. The smile would be in evidence only as long as the chin had its way, Kitty was sure. She felt herself blushing under the woman's frank, staring scrutiny.

"You are even more charming than was reported, Katherine," she exclaimed. "Mrs. Brampton," here she smiled and nodded at that lady, "hardly did you justice. If my fondest hopes are realized, my Christopher will be a very fortunate young man indeed." Somehow the note of complacent approval in the lady's voice failed to reassure Kitty.

"Christopher, do come forward and make your bow to Miss Leyburne. Isn't she quite as pretty as I told you?"

Kit stepped up to Kitty, rigidly correct, and bowed over her hand. "Charming, quite charming." Kitty was beginning to feel that she wasn't really there in the room—no one was talking as if she could hear them, and they were discussing her so openly. She hadn't dared to raise her eyes to see just what this young man looked like. She was afraid she would burst into tears if she did.

"We shall have the young people sit together on the love seat, don't you think that best, Mrs. de Fleming?" Mrs. Brampton said with a broad smile. Kitty knew that it was all well meant, but that was small comfort.

"The very thing! They must get to know one another."

Kitty could hear Kit heave a sigh of exasperation, then he bowed slightly again and gestured toward the seat. With a curtsey, she took it and they perched on the edge together, as far away from one another as was possible. A tray of lemonade and biscuits was brought in by Jameson and this filled a few awkward moments, as Mrs. Leyburne saw to the serving of each of her guests.

"I have been told that you are studying French, Katherine," Mrs. de Fleming said through crumbs. "I am pleased that you are such an accomplished young lady. The French language is the most elegant in the world and a knowledge of it adds an éclat of polish to one who is so fortunate."

"Thank you, Mrs. de Fleming."

"When you and Christopher get to know one another much better," she paused to titter, "you must learn to call me Mama, as he does. I hope that I shall soon stand in that position with you."

A frown from Mrs. Leyburne cut off whatever Kitty might have answered to this, for such a suggestion was extremely forward, not at all what she would have expected. "I am sure that Katherine will do all that is right and proper."

Kitty tried to eat a biscuit but couldn't make herself swallow the one tiny bite she had taken. Grabbing a glass of lemonade she took a deep drink and washed the biscuit down. There! At least she could talk clearly, if she must.

In an effort to revive the languishing conversation, Mrs. Brampton turned to Kit. "And you, Christopher, your mother has told me that you are very fond of horses."

He sputtered. "Fond of them?" Then his mother caught his eye and he hastened to agree. "Yes, quite fond of them." Hearing the dismay in his voice, Kitty stole a glance at him.

She saw a youth of nearly her own age, dressed in a waistcoat and neckcloth that struck her as inappropriately elaborate, even rather ludicrous, whose fair skin under the wavy brown locks had turned quite pink with embarrassment. He was every bit as uncomfortable as she. For a moment she forgot the broad shoulders of her officer, his air of poise and command, and took pity on Mr. de Fleming.

"My Papa has told me that you have a light, steady hand with a team, Mr. de Fleming," she murmured. Much of her conversation with that parent was centered on horses, and she was sure that at one time or another he could have said something of the sort.

Startled, Kit turned to stare at her for the first time. His expression seemed to say that he hadn't realized she was capable of more than polite responses to questions put to her, questions such as,

"More tea? Another crumpet?" It was as if one of his horses had spoken.

"You must call one another by your given names, children. Don't you agree, Mrs. Leyburne? With so much agreed to, they should be Katherine and Christopher to one another. We do so want them to be *friends.*"

She hesitated a moment, then said, "But of course. You are so right." She turned expectantly to her daughter, eyebrows raised as if to give encouragement, waiting.

Kitty looked at her in a panic, knowing what was expected of her but unwilling to give it. "Christopher." She barely managed to speak above a whisper, but this token of friendship pleased the three ladies immensely.

Kit was more grudging. He glared at his smiling mother for a moment, daring her to make him do this absurd thing, then resigned himself to it. "Katherine."

"There. That sounds so much better!" Both Mrs. Brampton and Mrs. de Fleming were beaming at the couple, sure that their matchmaking efforts were already beginning to bear fruit. Kit dove for the plate of biscuits, then remembered his manners in time and offered it to each of the ladies in turn before setting it down at the small table near his own place.

"I am so sorry that Mr. Leyburne was unable to join us for this little visit," their hostess apologized. "He was called away on business this morning and will be gone all day. We shall invite you to dine with us in a day or two, he is so anxious to meet you and Christopher, Mrs. de Fleming. He particularly wanted to get better acquainted before anything is definitely settled. . . ." She trailed off with embarrassment, for she knew that in the minds of the other ladies, everything *was* settled. To them the formal proposal would be but a gesture.

"I have had the honor of meeting Mr. Leyburne on many occasions," Mrs. de Fleming gushed. "He has always impressed me as the most kind and amiable of gentlemen. Christopher will be *so* fortunate to have him for a . . . But there, I have almost said too much again! We must speak of that in good time. But I know that Mr. Leyburne would be the kindest of mentors to my fatherless son."

"I have had the honor of meeting Mr. Leyburne, too, at Tattersall's purchasing a team," Kit suddenly declared, startling the mamas, who had almost forgotten their offsprings' presence. Kitty thought that he almost sounded human.

"Then you will agree with me that he is a most pleasant gentleman," his mother insisted before Kit could say more.

Kit paused. "Most pleasant. And he also knows a great deal about horseflesh," he ended defiantly.

Kitty rather thought that this latter point was more important to the young man than any amount of pleasant, amiable kindness. She felt herself sympathizing with him, despite her lack of interest in horses. Her father was dear to her because he loved her, and she him, and it pleased her that perhaps her chosen husband and the older man would have a common interest. She knew her father had always regretted the absence of a son.

"Excellent. Your acquaintanceship will undoubtedly grow into something closer, I am sure," his mother said.

"It is so nice that the two of you will share an enthusiasm," Mrs. Leyburne added. Kitty wondered if she had forgotten that Christopher was to marry her daughter, not her husband. She feared that a giggle was rising in her throat, the first sign of good humor she had felt since the awful news had been broken to her.

"I am so very pleased with you, Katherine," Mrs. de Fleming said as she leaned over to pat the girl's hand. "You are a most delightfully docile girl, quite well behaved. I do so dislike the manners of many of the young ladies being presented in recent years. They are most forward, pushing themselves into the notice of the Ton. It is quite pleasant to find that you are so dignified and demure. I am sure that Christopher agrees. Don't you, Christopher?"

"Of course," he said with a sigh. The giggle disappeared.

"I have trained my daughter along old-fashioned principles, Mrs. de Fleming. I have overseen every step of her education myself, choosing only the most qualified instructors and determining the curricula according to the strictest moral standards, such as I imbibed in my youth. I felt that that would be best for her. Even the most exclusive schools seem to have accepted an uncertain type of young lady today. I suppose that it is a sign of modern progress, but I can't help but regret it. I was most shocked when I investigated some of them, I assure you! Why, in one establishment, the children were actually allowed to use powder. Face powder! Imagine!"

Their talk continued in this vein for several minutes, the corruption of the modern generation always a fascinating topic to its elders. The two young people were left sitting on the sofa, forgotten once again. They were side by side, never looking at one another, acknowledging the other's presence only insofar as it was necessary to reach for a biscuit. They were startled when a word from Mrs. de Fleming told them that they were once again under consideration.

"It is going to be a fine day, I am sure. You two children must get out and enjoy some fresh air and a brisk walk."

"Yes, of course," Mrs. Leyburne agreed. "I will just ring for Carter to accompany you." She reached for the bellpull and tugged it vigorously. The door opened immediately to show Carter with a cloak and bonnet for Kitty. The maid dropped a curtsey and stood just inside the door.

"Yes, the Park is quite near. It will make a pleasant stroll for the two of them," Mrs. Brampton said. "Do run along, children, and enjoy yourselves. You must use this opportunity to get better acquainted with one another."

Reluctantly, Kit and Kitty rose to their feet. Kitty curtseyed to the ladies, murmured the appropriate words, and hurried over to the comforting presence of her maid.

Kit was bowing over his mother's hand when that lady's voice rang out across the room. "You know what is expected of you, Christopher. I have told you what to say. Make good use of your time."

Then she reached up to pat his arm, her mouth spread in a beaming smile.

Scarlet-faced, Kit and Kitty left the room, each avoiding the other's eyes.

Four

To Kitty's chagrin, the young man beside her chose to follow the path, her very special path on which she always lingered, hoping to catch sight of her cavalier. Worried at what He would think if he caught sight of her with another, she glanced quickly around the greenery, ready to turn and run, faint, or do whatever she must to keep from being seen. While her charged emotions created turmoil in her breast, her escort walked stoically by her side, whether because of his own pre-occupations or because of the courtesy he considered due a member of the weaker sex, setting a very slow pace. Carter followed at a discreet distance.

It should have been an ideal setting for a romantic interlude. The sun, having dispelled a light mist that morning, was shining triumphantly. Birds sang, flowers bloomed, and happy strollers and riders filled the paths. There was even a semblance of privacy as one followed the path through the shrubbery and trees that lined its route. At times there was only Kitty's faithful maid to see and hear what, if anything, passed between the two young people.

Young Mr. de Fleming seemed to gather himself to speak to Kitty, and she braced herself. He opened his mouth several times. "Miss Leyburne, I do not recall a more lovely day in the Park," he finally offered.

"Yes, it is quite lovely," she mumbled into the handle of her parasol.

"Lovely. Yes, lovely."

They walked further.

"Do you know the Park well?" he ventured.

With a start, she turned her reddening face away. "Yes, quite well. I walk here often."

"To see friends?"

"Friends? Whatever can you mean?" The clandestine daydreams came to mind, dreams of walking and talking and riding with a certain military gentleman.

"Why, with other young ladies, school friends, I don't know what I mean!" he snapped peevishly.

"Oh. Yes, well, I'm afraid I know so few people here in London, Mr. de Fleming. There are few people to enjoy the Park with. I come here often with Carter, my maid. We have explored the paths many a day."

"Kit!" he said with a sudden excess of audacity.

"Kit?"

"You must call me Kit. Everyone does. It's short for Christopher."

It was on the tip of Kitty's tongue to ask if his mama had told him to invite her to do so. Surely she must be the source of authority for so daring an offering. Then another thought, a rather silly and daunting one, came to mind.

"Oh, dear."

"What's wrong?" His voice was peevish again, even a trifle defensive, but she failed to catch these nuances. "Is there something amiss, Miss Leyburne?"

"Kitty."

"Kitty?" Now he was angry. "I am called Kit, not Kitty, like some feline or a young girl or a . . ."

"No! *I* am Kitty."

"Oh!"

They had stopped in the middle of the path as they tried to untangle this matter of appellations, blocking the way of whoever might be passing along it. As luck would have it, their dismayed, almost resentful stares were interrupted by the necessity of stepping aside for a heavy-set dowager of uncertain years. That good lady, more sensitive to expression than either of the youngsters, cast a sharp glance at each of them, then noticed Carter lingering but a few paces away and lost interest. The young people resumed their walk.

Without noticing what she was doing, Kitty had begun to move at her normal pace, one that was considerably livelier than the gentle stroll Kit had deemed suitable. In a moment she had outpaced him.

"Please don't be angry!"

The words came from behind her and she spun around to see that Kit was hurrying to catch up with her, an expression of embarrassment and contrition on his face.

"I didn't mean to be rude to you, truly I didn't. It is just that this is such a damnable situation . . ." Shocked with his own license, he stumbled to a halt. "I shouldn't have—I mean—to say such a . . !"

She ignored his confusion. "And embarrassing. All of it." She flashed a smile at him.

This time they were able to walk at a pace agreeable to both of them, interrupted by the necessity to stop and stare at one another.

"I should not have used such a word, please believe me that I am mortified that such a word should have escaped my lips in the presence of a lady!"

"Oh, pooh! My papa uses it all the time when he doesn't like something."

"Yes, well, it is not that I don't like something, that is . . ."

"Yes, you do. You don't like the idea of marrying me; your mama insists." She paused and then hinted daringly, "You would rather choose another."

He studied the small stones beneath their feet for some moments before he answered. "As does yours."

"Yes, she does, doesn't she? She and my godmother, Mrs. Brampton, they are both quite determined. I do believe that Mrs. Brampton is the most determined woman alive."

"Yes, I have heard of her."

"And her money, too, I suppose. Everyone seems

to know that it is to come to me in time," Kitty said with a touch of bitterness.

Kit's face was still scarlet with embarrassment, but he braced himself to give an honest answer. "Yes, they do. There has been rather a lot of talk, you know."

"It's all her fault! I was perfectly happy up in Cumberland, studying with the rector and Papa. It was Mrs. Brampton who sent for me and is insisting on this coming out and the Season, and—and . . ."

"And this marriage?"

Close to tears, Kitty nodded her head. "I wish she would keep her old money."

"What!" Kit, well versed in the necessities of aristocratic life, was deeply shocked. "How can you say such a thing? Why, fifty thousand pounds is enough to assure you a life of comfort and ease. You can command all the elegancies with such a fortune!"

"I was comfortable at home."

"But you will be a rich woman, independent!"

"Independent? How can you say that?"

"You will never be beholden to richer relatives or dunning tradesmen or any of that!"

"And will I be able to do what I want? Isn't that what independence means?"

He thought for a moment. "Oh, I see."

"And you, you will have a title some day. That will enable you to sit in the House of Lords, to help govern the country. Yet see what is has done for you! You can't even choose your own wife, a right any commoner would exercise without a second thought." The spirit of rebellion was rising in her, a rebellion she would have never dreamed of but an hour before. *She* would not accept this loveless match! She would oppose this wedding in every way she knew how.

These were new thoughts to Kit, new and strange ones. He had never seen his situation in such a dismal light before, and the sphere of politics had never appealed to him. What did he care about government? He had always done what was right and proper. Then the recollection that he couldn't marry the woman he loved in any case returned to him, and his thoughts took to their more usual channels, ones well defined by others.

"We must accept our obligations," he proclaimed.

"Pooh!"

"No, we must. I shall inherit estates that require my care and attention. There are people who look to me for leadership and support, or they will some day. I must be sensible about all this."

It is likely that Kitty would have continued to argue the point, for she had plucked his sleeve in some agitation and turned to him with an animated face. But then disaster, the disaster she had feared and planned to avoid, overtook her. Out of the corner of her eye she saw a familiar figure.

There, on his fine stallion, his head bare as he stared across the verge into her eyes, a sorrowing look on his face, sat her officer. He had taken a position beneath an oak tree, the one where she often lingered when the afternoon sun became too bright, and she had not seen him yet on his ride. From under the tree he would have had an excellent view of her walk with Kit de Fleming, their animated conversation, and the fact that Kitty was clinging to him in a most familiar manner. His thoughts were written on his face, clear for her to read.

"Oh! Oh, no, but . . . !" Snatching her hand away from the arm beside her, Kitty raised it to her flaming cheek.

"Yes, you see, I am right!" Kit insisted as if there had been a lengthy argument between them, successfully concluded in his favor "One must be practical, not sentimental, about such things. One is born into a station in life, and one must accept what it brings with it, good and bad. It is the price we pay."

The officer slowly replaced his hat on his glowing hair, then, head bowed, he turned his horse away from the occupied path and struck out across the grass. To Kitty's horror, he cast not one backward glance over his shoulder.

Kit failed to notice her lack of attention. "Can one turn one's back on one's heritage? No! One must accept the ways of the world. *We* must accept them!" He had been swept along by his borrowed eloquence and took her silence for assent. Emboldened, he grabbed her unwilling hand and pressed it within his. "And so you see, Miss Leyburne, Kitty, we must accept what fate has presented to us. I have the deepest regard for you. You are a lovely young lady, one I am sure that I shall come to hold in the highest—uh—regard. Esteem! The highest esteem! Please, won't you allow us to become better acquainted? I'm sure we shall rub along together tolerably well. Why don't we give this scheme a try?"

The horseman had disappeared. Kitty, her hopes shattered, lowered her head. A jubilant Kit, ill-versed in the ways of young ladies, mistook this for maidenly acquiesence and sighed with relief.

"There, that wasn't so bad after all. Was it?" Pleased with himself, he turned toward the Park entrance and started for home.

As the young people were approaching Kitty's home, a certain interesting gentleman was returning his borrowed mount to a brother officer.

"Dash it all, I have the dam'est luck!" he complained to his friend. "I was just playing her in nicely, you know, she'd grabbed the bait, I'm sure, when the next thing I know, someone else steals a march on me! Another heiress gone west, old boy! I shall have to find me another."

Five

"So you intend they make a match of it?"

"But of course! It's everything we've hoped for! Imagine, a title *and* a fortune," Mrs. Leyburne trilled.

"Harrumph!"

Somewhat daunted by the disgruntled sound of this, she held her tongue. Mr. Leyburne filled his pipe with maddening deliberation, then continued. "The title is his by law, unless the old man begets a son of his own."

"But surely not, not at his age!"

He ignored her. "And considering his feelings for that jumped-up niece-in-law of his, he just may try it! There is no surety that he will leave the money to the lad. That is his own, earned by his own hand and his to dispose of as he pleases."

"When one stops to think of *how* he earned it! If you can say that he did!"

"No more of that!" His voice was forbidding. "You know how I feel on that topic. You should not listen to that fool de Fleming woman."

"Well, putting *that* aside, of course Christopher will come into the fortune, surely the law will see to that!"

"Not at all. Only the title is entailed, my dear. And some of the estate, but that must cost a fortune to maintain."

"Is that true? How unfair! To be able to leave your property away from your own flesh and blood, from those nearest and dearest to one" (her husband winced at this), "from those who have a natural and rightful claim to it! Preposterous! And besides," she added with candor, "there's no one else for him to leave it to!"

"It has happened. Mrs. Brampton being a case in point."

His wife preferred to ignore this jibe. "Do you mean it could really happen?"

"The money may go to the local alms house, or whatever else catches his fancy."

"That is immoral, indecent! Improper! No one could contemplate doing such a thing!"

"That old man could. After all, he's been accused of worse, far worse, in his day, and by those whom one would think 'nearest and dearest,' those from whom he could be said to have every claim of consideration." He waited for her to reply.

"Whatever can you be speaking of?"

"That niece-in-law of his is quick enough to

spread evil of him. Could you blame him if he chooses to leave his money elsewhere?"

"Surely not! She would never, he would . . ." She trailed off into sputters. What he said was true enough. Mrs. de Fleming had been far from discreet regarding her husband's kinsman and her opinion of certain of his activities. Alleged activities. And such things had been known to happen, Mrs. Brampton being an example close to home, although that lady had naught but a distant cousin to lay claim to.

But this turn of thought proved a happy one and she announced triumphantly, "They will have Kitty's money to live on, even if that wicked old man ignores every tenet of decency and morality and keeps his old money! Kitty will have quite enough for the two of them!"

He suddenly looked up from his pipe and smiled at her. "That may well be true. There will be something coming to her from us one day, too."

The conversation had come back full circle. "And so you see that it is really an excellent scheme, this match. Kitty has a fortune and breeding, perhaps not the grand connections such as some girls can claim but enough that young Christopher needn't be ashamed for her!"

"And he has a title," her husband concluded good-naturedly. "Just what you, and Mrs. Brampton, have had your hearts set on all these years!"

"Exactly! Imagine, our daughter a countess!"

She turned to him, her eyes alight with excitement, but on catching sight of the expression on his face, sighed impatiently. "Why must you become so dour of a sudden? Now what flaw have you found?"

He took her gently by the hand and pulled her into his lap. "It may require more than a title to make our Kitty a happy woman for the rest of her life, my dear."

"What can you be saying? Surely a title is what every young girl wants."

"What she may want, and what she should have for a lifetime of happy marriage are two separate things. At least, that has been my observation of young girls. And I am not altogether sure that Kitty does want this title."

"Such foolishness!" She tried to twist out of his lap, but he had her firm in his arms. "And I am not even sure she is old enough to know her own mind."

"Then we must know it for her."

"She is young enough and romantic enough to seek love, my very own love. Have you forgotten your own girlhood? Our courtship?"

His wife was blushing becomingly but hid her head in his shoulder before he could do more than appreciate a glimpse of it. "But to be Lady Helm some day! Surely?"

He shook his head no.

"Have I made a terrible mistake? Is that what you are telling me?"

"No, not at all. I wouldn't have let things go this far if I thought that. Let us examine this proposed marriage from a more rational point of view."

"Yes, dear." She curled her feet under her and prepared to listen.

"This young Kit seems to be a nice enough lad."

"Very nice."

"His own background, the wicked uncle aside, seems sound enough as to family and education."

"Oh, yes, the best schools!"

"He is of an age with Kitty."

"Nearly to the day!"

"Well . . ."

"Close enough. And his family and ours are from the same part of the world. He will be familiar with the same people, know the district, fall into the way of life."

"Well . . ."

"Well? Now I am in error?" she asked.

"Never that! But he has spent the whole of his life here in London and attended schools in the south, except for some very brief times in the north. I fear you will find his knowledge of Cumberland sadly deficient."

"Well, it must be in his blood, surely?"

"Surely it is!" he agreed.

She glanced up at him from his shoulder, the movement timid and furtive. When he saw her glance he smiled and dropped a kiss on her forehead. "Yes, another thought?"

"No, my dear, just an old one. It seems that you are willing to encourage this match after all, as I had hoped. Am I right?"

"You are right. But I will not have Kitty forced into an engagement where there is no attachment on her side, nor on the young man's, for that matter."

"Of course not! To force them to marry would be positively Gothic! Every feeling must revolt!"

"You might try explaining that to Mrs. Brampton!" Then seeing her abashed face, he relented. "So we must give them a chance to get better acquainted and hope for the best." Then there came to him the image of a chic new equipage he had seen bowling through the Park and fashionable streets of London, along with the whisperings heard of who had paid for Lady Madge's latest extravagances. His face settled into sterner lines. "And so I would suggest that we take some action to ensure that opportunity."

"Whatever can you mean?"

"Merely this. That we should get the young people away from London, and its myriad attractions and distractions."

"But the Season has not yet begun!"

"It will do them no harm, they will have other Seasons to enjoy. And besides, if this match becomes a fact, young Kit will be assuming some new responsibilities that will weigh more heavily on his shoulders than the purchase of nags at Tattersall's. There is no reason why he shouldn't know what they are before an irrevocable decision is reached."

"Responsibilities?"

"Kitty is my only child. My property will go to her one day, and it will be her husband's duty to manage it. Kit ought to see where part of his future with Kitty would lie. I shan't have my land going into the hands of a wastrel or worse. I've worked too hard to countenance such a thing! I must take my own measure of this Kit and see if he is up to snuff."

"Wastrel? How can you use such a term against

that charming young man? He is everything that is courteous and kind! You must be teasing me!"

"I'm sure he is everything you say. But he is only just beginning to spread his wings. I want to see which direction he'll take. Yes, I think a visit north is called for."

Six

It was Mrs. Brampton who unwittingly effected Mr. Leyburne's suggestion that the young couple be separated from London.

The prospect of her goddaughter advantageously connected to the scion of an old and noble house thrilled her. But the aforementioned scion had the unfortunate habit of slipping away from her presence, and that of his fiancée, with disconcerting regularity. Mrs. Brampton had too good an opinion of herself to guess that he might hold her in personal distaste, so she ascribed this lack of courtesy to the temptations of the metropolis. She set about with her usual energy to remedy the trouble. Transported to a scene over which she exercised her beneficent control, she was sure that she would soon have young de Fleming behaving exactly as he should.

"It would be such an honor for me to be the first to fete the young couple, Mrs. Leyburne," she confided to that lady over a private tea one rainy afternoon.

Mrs. Leyburne, aware of the strictures placed on her by her husband, was dismayed by this assumption that all was settled between her daughter and Kit de Fleming.

"It is very kind of you to offer such a treat, but truly, my dear Mrs. Brampton, it is too much for us to ask of you!" But before she could enlarge on her theme, the other lady continued with her own thoughts.

"We shall announce their betrothal from Broughton Place, my dear friend. What could be more proper? More dignified? We would thus avoid the crush and notoriety that such an interesting event would undoubtedly incur here in London, giving it all the advantages of a small and intimate occasion, quite *en famille,* you know. It is so much more exclusive that way."

"My husband . . ."

"Mr. Leyburne will undoubtedly want to inspect his own estates while so far north. I shall not be offended if he chooses to travel on to the Hall." A sensible woman, she had no illusions of where she stood in Mr. Leyburne's esteem.

"He has not precisely given his consent to this match!"

"It wants but a little delicate handling and all will be settled. Leave it in my hands, dear friend! I shall see to it all. You must trust me!"

"He—I mean—we had thought to let the young

couple grow better acquainted with one another. . . ."

"As they will at Broughton, I doubt not. In fact, that was precisely my intention, Mrs. Leyburne! Precisely! What the situation requires is privacy and adroit planning by those who are sympathetic and interested. Such as I! A female of my experience and station in life is best qualified to achieve all that we want. You need have no fear of my enthusiasm in this matter."

It was not Mrs. Brampton's enthusiasm that Mrs. Leyburne doubted—far from it. She was aware that the other lady had every reason to desire the happy arrangement of a marriage between her goddaughter and young de Fleming. It would be the culmination of a long-standing ambition that had been carefully nurtured through the years of scrambling on the fringes of society, then slowly penetrating the outer circles. Mrs. Brampton undoubtedly saw herself poised on the verge of entering the inner sanctums of the haut Ton through this connection with so august a name as de Fleming.

For you see, Mrs. Leyburne's doubts rose from Mrs. Brampton's claim to a station in life. It was true that she was a perfectly estimable woman, the daughter of a country vicar in a parish near Leyburne Hall. It was not a church which the Leyburnes attended themselves, their abode being in another parish. It was only the merest chance that had brought them there on the very day their first (and as events later proved, their only) child was born, some two months before it was due.

Retiring to the nearest substantial residence, the rectory, Mrs. Leyburne had been delivered of an undersized girl, one so puny that all had entertained lurid doubts as to the mite's ability to long survive in this world. It was this fear, coupled with the peculiar convenience of a religious man so near at hand, that had inspired the parents to have their daughter baptized immediately following her birth. And necessity and the sacrament demanding a godmother, they had seized what was available, the vicar's daughter, a worthy maid affianced to an up-and-coming merchant from Kendal. So it was that Mrs. Brampton, then Miss Cuthby, had achieved such a degree of intimacy with the Leyburne family. Mr. Brampton's amazing success in trade had done the rest.

"You must not hesitate to leave it all to me, as you have done so many times before! I know just how it all ought to be done, never fear!"

Mrs. Leyburne writhed under this assurance. She had, all too often, done precisely that, and she had vivid memories of the results of some of those decisions. She gathered the courage to oppose in some way her strong-willed companion.

"Mr. Leyburne is most particular that no announcement be made immediately. That must be understood."

"Oh, perfectly, perfectly!" Mrs. Brampton's indulgent smile showed how seriously she took all of this. "The gentlemen have so little understanding of these peculiarly female concerns, they will have their little qualms and whims! I'll wager that once it is all settled, he will have little enough to say!"

"He shall discover any announcement made without his approval, that is certain."

Her hostess merely shook her head, smiled, and clucked her tongue.

"It would mean a retraction in the *Times*. If necessary."

This drew the other woman's attention for the first time. "Surely not! He could not mean to do such a thing!"

"Oh, but he could and he would!"

"But the scandal!"

"It would mean little or nothing to him! You know him!"

Mrs. Brampton was positively shaken at the thought. "It could ruin us all! Young Kitty, too! It would put an end to any hope of a respectable match for her!"

"Such would be a small matter to him. He would expect the rest of the world to be as tolerant and forgetful as he!"

"A retraction! Well, really. I must think on that. A retraction!"

And think she did for the remainder of the meal, so much so that the projected visit to Broughton Place was nearly forgotten. Alas for Mrs. Leyburne's peace of mind, and the comfort of many, this did not quite happen.

"We shall see what Mr. Leyburne has to say after we have all retired to Cumberland, my dear Mrs. Leyburne! We shall see!" This proclamation was delivered with a straight back and a gleaming eye, and Mrs. Leyburne, her presentiment based on long experience, suffered a secret sigh and a shudder to escape her.

So it was arranged over tea that a se'night hence the Brampton and Leyburne carriages, filled with those families and their guests, would set out for the north. Any suggestion that Mrs. de Fleming would raise objections against a project that would take her from London at the start of the Season were swept aside, with some justice. After all, Mrs. Brampton was no mean judge of character, at least not in those areas influenced by the judicious expenditure of money.

They would linger indefinitely at Broughton Place, the Brampton country seat only recently improved by Mrs. Brampton's taste coupled with Mr. Brampton's money. There, all the principals involved would be under the roof and eye, not to say the personality and influence, of Mrs. Brampton herself. And that lady had no doubts, no fears whatever, of her ability to achieve an outcome that would satisfy to a nicety her own desires.

Having achieved so much, at least in the planning stage, Mrs. Brampton was gracious enough to agree that it would be fitting, and pleasing to Mr. Leyburne, that the party would at some time after the announcement of the engagement travel even further north to Leyburne Hall, there to enjoy the hospitality of the bride-to-be's family. After all, young Kit should begin to acquaint himself with what would one day undoubtedly be his through his wife, and Mr. Leyburne was a force to appease and reckon with. By the time the last crumb of plum cake had been rescued from its solitary position on the plate, the matter was settled.

* * *

When Mr. Leyburne was told of the visit, he merely shrugged his shoulders and set about making plans for his own convenience. He would depart for the north two days before the ladies were to set out in their cavalcade, travel straight to his own property of Leyburne Hall, there to arrange for the eventual arrival of his wife and guests. He had one eye on avoiding Mrs. Brampton and the other on circumventing her interference.

Mrs. de Fleming, pleased by this mark of support and honor for the match coming as it did from so formidable a power, welcomed Mrs. Brampton's plans as she would those of a valued ally.

Kitty, who had sought in vain for one last glimpse of her cavalier, felt only indifference that she would not be deprived of all hope of seeing him again. Even the lure of her beloved meres and fells failed to stimulate her interest, much to her mother's chagrin. That good lady could not know that, at the advanced age of seventeen, her daughter had given up all hope of ever being happy again.

It was Kit, with so much more to leave behind in London, who was distraught when he heard the announcement of the trip. An interview with Lady Madge did little to relieve the emotions which burdened his soul. The sense of his impending loss, however temporary, of the lady's company immediately drove him to her side.

"But we shall be apart only in the flesh, dearest Kit!" she protested in the face of his anger and disappointment.

"That is precisely the point!"

"In spirit we shall never be separated, my darling. They can never do that!" Despite a momentary flare of irritation, she could not help but preen herself with this display of his devotion.

Kit, for the first time impatient for her romantic and foolish notions, waved this aside with an impatient gesture. "I am sure that the spirit will take care of itself quite nicely when we are able to see one another, speak to one another, touch . . ."

"We shall be in touch, Kit! We shall write letters every day, recording all that has happened in the other's absence, all that our souls have felt. And besides, you will be so pleased with the Lake District! One cannot help but envy you the opportunity! It is all the thing now, you know, and they say that this man Brampton has been quite lavish when it came to building his very own country seat. All will be in the height of luxury."

"I don't care for my own comfort, much less luxury! I would surrender it all to be with you, you know that!"

"Yes, darling, but the Lake District is said to be so very beautiful! Everyone is visiting it now, talking about it, wanting to go there! You will enjoy it immensely, I'm sure. I quite envy you your journey."

Kit seized on this idea. "Why don't you follow me? You could stay nearby, some place close enough for us to meet daily. I cannot bear to think of being away from you!"

"Stay some place nearby? Wherever can you mean? I, stay at some shabby inn? Or take rooms with some yokels? Surely you cannot be in earnest! You are jesting, tell me it is so!"

"But we could be together still! Isn't that what's important?"

"You in luxury, me in shabby lodgings?"

"I would gladly reverse our positions, just to be near you, darling Madge!" He took her hand, covering it with kisses. With her other she gently stroked the curls of his hair, noticing with pleasure how the sun played on the magnificent diamond that adorned her hand.

"Our souls will be as one, darling. Can you doubt it, you in the most beautiful district in the whole of England? The most romantic, the most picturesque, the most aesthetically pleasing? And I, here in London, longing for you with all my heart? Besides, you must think of the scandal there would be if I followed you north!"

Angered, Kit jumped to his feet, trapping her hands in his with a ferocious grip. Such were his feelings that he must vent them with argument and bitter recrimination. The excuse was literally at hand.

"You have a new ring, I see. A new jewel! You have found another lover, someone else has replaced me in your affections! You are accepting gifts from another man, aren't you?"

Lady Madge smiled her slow, sweet smile, shaking her head in patient denial. It had been slow coming, this jealousy and anger, but she had known it would appear at some point. It had happened always before this way. Whatever the truth of the accusation, she knew what she would say. "It is but a tawdry bauble, one I've had these many years. What you take for a gemstone is merely paste. Do calm yourself, my dearest, silliest love! As if I could ever love another than you."

And with suave words and loving gestures, she turned away his anger and disappointment and soon led him to accept the inevitability—and rightness—of the journey and its planned result.

Seven

The land between the south of England and the Lake District gradually changes over the miles until the traveler cannot but guess that he has departed one country and entered into an alien land, so great are the differences to be found. From flat tidewater lands one moves into splendid mountains. The gentle hills of the Home Counties embrace the eastern plain of the island, it is true, but the spine of the country is the Pennine Chain, bristling along its central length and abetted by the smaller clusters of higher ground to the south. The Chilterns and the Cotswolds imbedded in the gut of the land to the southwest are but hints of the Pennines, for these latter are more truly a mountain range, a chain of peaks and valleys such as one finds in Europe or on other continents. They are like a stiff fence between east and west, while the southern heights are merely clustered mounds.

The party had traveled almost due north on leaving London, for it was along the eastern plain that Mrs. Brampton claimed the most friends and connections, her father's vocation standing her in good stead. He had served as curate of two parishes and later rector of another before he had moved to the north. If the principle house in a district wasn't open to Mrs. Brampton, she could rely on the rectory for hospitality, but it was rare that the latter was called for. Years of wealth and a taste for travel had long since opened many doors to that lady, the rectory connection at times providing the wedge she needed. Now, with two certifiable aristocrats in her charge, for the de Fleming name was a well-known one, and with the Leyburnes, who were, after all, of old gentry stock, she was showing off one world to the other. London friends could be impressed with the range of her connections in the provinces, the provincial hosts could enjoy the touch of glamour and prestige that came with providing bed and board to a future lord. The journey, a night here, two there, was in the nature of a triumphal progress, the group passing from fete to fete.

Kit detested it all.

He had soon come to appreciate Mr. Leyburne's desire for haste. Kitty's father had set out as planned, despite his wife's protests and Mrs. Brampton's complaisance with his absence. Thus he had avoided hours of boring chatter in a closed coach with a woman of small education and even smaller mind, chatter clearly intended to bind young Kit to her influence. Chatter followed by dull evenings and occasionally days spent in labored amiability with strangers who were decent enough folk, but not the sort he would have sought if left to himself. Days of slow, plodding progress that tripled the length of the journey Mr. Leyburne had undoubtedly long since completed, traveling as he was—light and fast and not restricted by two coaches and a following chaise. Kit was hard pressed to cling to his peace of mind in the circumstances; he was ashamed of his occasional flashes of anger and impatience. Only the knowledge that Lady Madge, as well as his mother and this meddling woman, had wished the horror of this journey on him enabled him to maintain a semblance of calm.

From York Mrs. Brampton lead her party in a path almost due west across the Pennines. This was Kit's first opportunity to inspect the countryside so far north. His mother had long since quarreled with his father's family, and the decease of that gentleman meant that there was no more exchange between his widow and his relations, for there was no one to perform the role of mediator and peacemaker. Kit had last traveled into Cumberland as a child of eight. It would be expected that his youthful memories of the mountains would be greatly exaggerated in estimating their true size, for after all, he had been so much smaller in relation to their grandeur then, but it was with a detached surprise and appreciative eye that he watched the contours of the land take on steeper and steeper folds, rising ever upward into what must be the highest peaks in the British Isles.

Surely a range of such magnitude, one that divided the country east from west, would boast the highest altitude?

It was Kitty who corrected this impression, giving the honor where it was due. Between outbursts of gossip and inane innuendo regarding their coming happy situation, the couple, sharing as they did the foremost coach with Mrs. Brampton during much of the journey, were able to exchange some innocuous comments. For the first time Kit began to appreciate that Miss Leyburne was quite a good sort, despite the machinations of those around her.

"You see, they say Scafell Peak is the highest point in England."

"Scafell?"

"Yes, but a few miles from my home."

"But the map shows no great range of hills, only a jumble of highlands."

"But out of that jumble comes the tallest mountain."

He shook his head. "It doesn't seem right."

"If you would care to ask another . . . !"

"No, no, I don't doubt your word, it's just that one would hope for a more suitable setting for such grandeur."

"Perhaps the Pennines are grander at first sight, they march in so straight an order, but the fells and pikes of the Cumberland area have a beauty of their own in the precision of their arrangement. Everything is so perfectly to scale that it all *seems* bigger."

"An ill-assorted jumble . . ."

"But home to me. And to you, I recollect? Isn't Helm Pele your ancestral seat?"

He started and a flush rose on his face, but before he could answer Mrs. Brampton's eyes flew open and she ceased her game of 'possum to take part in the talk.

"Mr. de Fleming has spent little time here in the north, Kitty. I am sure that he does not think of it as home in the least, not in the least. It would not be natural if he did, having spent so much of his life in the south. Although this is not to say that he will not be very taken with what he shall see, eh, young man?" She poked his booted calf with the top of her foot and nodded approval of her opinion. Kit could do no more than smile and nod back, but he could not bring himself to be hearty about her presumption. He *was* relieved in the change in subject.

Kitty had half guessed that Mrs. Brampton's many little naps were nothing more than a subterfuge, an attempt to let the young people talk and get acquainted, giving that lady an opportunity to follow it all while not seeming, in fact, to spy. This interruption confirmed her guess. She glanced at Kit, but all she could see was his profile, still flushed; he had taken a sudden interest in the countryside they were passing through. Kitty knew that she had stumbled onto delicate ground; just how, she wasn't sure. With typical determination, she set her heart on knowing more of this secret, and turned her mind to ways of achieving this.

Kit was the obvious source of information. Once settled in Broughton Place, she guessed that she would have increased opportunity to draw him out on the subject. It was clearly part of their elders' plans that they should have time together, presumably to become better friends. She spared an unspoken word of thanks for her father, for she knew that the responsibility for this consideration rested squarely on his shoulders. She vowed to discover more from Kit, or if that failed, from the people of her home district, for the Pele was but a few miles distant from the Hall.

While her mind wove plots and subterfuges for uncovering the information her curiosity craved, she reserved for her godmother a demure silence. Mrs. Brampton's interruption had been all too opportune; Kitty guessed that lady would not approve of whatever the secret was. And as always, the less Mrs. Brampton knew, the better for the comfort of all concerned, herself most of all.

Eight

Mrs. Brampton considered her home to be a prime piece of the history of the area. In fact, she thought of herself, through her husband, as descending from one of the local heroes.

"For you see, Brampton is but a corruption of Broughton," she explained for the first but by no means last time over breakfast the day after they had arrived. "And so, of course, Mr. Brampton is descended from brave Sir Thomas."

"Sir Thomas?" Kit expressed his ignorance with a civil show of interest.

"Sir Thomas Broughton! He was driven from Witherslack Hall after Lambert Simnel's Rebellion."

"Lambert . . . ?" She had clearly lost him.

"Sir Thomas supported Simnel's claim to the

throne, and when the cause was lost, Sir Thomas was outlawed!"

"He sounds a ruffian of the worst sort!" Kit said warmly, missing the tenor of the lady's tale and somewhat confused. "I would have thought that loyalty to the crown would be the duty of every right-thinking gentleman."

"Do let Mrs. Brampton complete her tale, Kit," his mother protested, correctly interpreting their hostess's expression. She wanted peace, despite her own mood, now sulky in the extreme after rising at so early an hour. She was more accustomed to skipping breakfast altogether.

Having chosen to ignore Kit's ill-timed common sense, Mrs. Brampton continued. "Sir Thomas lived in a cave nearby. We shall be visiting it tomorrow, never fear, and you shall have a chance to see it for yourselves. It is most impressive. And his loyal tenants provided him with food and the necessities of life. It was but a bare survival!" She paused over her bacon, enjoying a delicate shudder over the thought of such hardship.

"A sad tale," Mrs. Leyburne murmured into her eggs. She was relieved after all that her husband had traveled on ahead, for she knew what his reaction to Mrs. Brampton's etymology would be. He had no sympathy, only contempt, for her theory of the root of her commonplace husband's name, and this social affectation disgusted him. If nothing else, he would have pointed out that Sir Thomas died without issue, which would raise all sorts of indelicate speculation.

"A touching story! When he died some years later they buried him in Witherslack Wood in an unmarked grave that has been remembered ever since. The local people point it out one generation to the other! And you shall never guess our good fortune!" She had gathered the attention of everyone at the table.

"Yes, and what might that be?" Kitty inquired after a lengthy silence.

"The grave is right here on our very property! It was one reason that I urged Mr. Brampton to purchase this land and build here. This way he is able to honor his ancestor's memory with the memorial dignities appropriate to his bravery. Isn't that fine of him?"

"But I thought that all trace of the grave had been lost!" Kitty protested.

Mrs. de Fleming snorted in a most unladylike fashion, but Mrs. Brampton chose to ignore this. She also ignored Kitty's comment.

"We are having a little memorial monument erected on the site so that Sir Thomas will always be remembered and revered as he ought. We had planned a little ceremony, a sort of service, to consecrate it in a week or two, with the local vicar officiating. Friends will be coming up for the event."

Everyone was studiously examining their plates as this announcement was delivered, everyone except Kit. If what the girl said was true, if the grave site was lost, then this was an impertinent piece of self-puffing flummery. Without the benefit of Mr. Leyburne's wider experience, he too suspected that the name Brampton had its origins in something other than Broughton, try though his hostess would. He glanced over at his mother, wondering what the reaction of so superior a sensibility would be to this foolishness. He had often heard her criticize, and on occasion deflate, this very sort of pretension in London society.

"A pretty thought," she said with a forced smile. "And the name Witherslack? How quaint! What is its origin? I have surely never heard anything like it before."

"Yes, it does add to the picturesque quality of our little home. We may not have a mere, but we do have some fine views of the fells, and the especial interest of family history to make this neighborhood all very dear to us!"

"How lovely."

"There are other names of interest here about," Kitty offered. "Cowmire Hall, for one."

"I wonder you do not call your place Witherslack Hall, Mrs. Brampton," Mrs. de Fleming said in an excess of affability. "It is so picturesque a name, you should seize on it!"

A long silence ensued. "There is another Witherslack Hall but a few miles distant," Mrs. Brampton at last explained. "It would not do to duplicate an older name still in use." Then with better humor she added, "And besides, it is not the family name. Broughton is our connection with the place, and so Broughton Place we have named it." And with that piece of wit she glanced around the table, waiting for the applause of her guests. She received an embarrassed smile from the two ladies and was favored with a view of the tops of the young peoples' heads.

Kit, stirring his ham around on his plate, wondered if this was to set the tone for the whole of the visit. If so, it would be intolerable. Broughton Place indeed! Whatever could be inspiring his mother to tolerate such an encroaching mushroom? He had never seen her behave so before. Things couldn't get much worse, he was sure.

They could. Despite its location to the south of the important meres, Kendal is considered by many the gateway to the Lake Counties. There is much to recommend it and its environs to the discriminating visitor and many pass through there on their way to the well-known beauty spots of the District. So it was fitting that it was near Kendal that Kit and Kitty received their first taste of the attitude of these southern tourists when visiting the grandeur of Cumberland and Westmoreland. At Broughton they met Lakers.

The lady's appropriation of local history was but a hint of what was to come. In her eagerness to advance her social position, Mrs. Brampton would have herself known as a lavish hostess. With such a history to enjoy, how could she not share it? She needed subjects. On hearing that some acquaintances from London were staying nearby, she insisted that they frequent her home, giving the excuse that the young people needed amusement. It was also pleasant to show to them the real live heir to a title who was staying under her very roof.

It was Kit's first exposure to the foibles of the Lakers, those visitors from other parts of the British Isles and as far afield as Europe, who came to the northwest of England to admire the scenery. They followed in the footsteps of Thomas

Grey, William Wordsworth, and others of lesser note and talent, often holding the illustrated guide to the Lake District compiled by Mr. Ackermann. They were precious, unimaginative, and very dull to his way of thinking. They admired the same scenes that Mr. Ackermann recommended, viewing them from the stations or vantage points he pointed out, and praised them in terms supplied by Mrs. Radcliffe and other contributors to the book. Kit often wondered that they ever bothered to leave their warm fires and easychairs in London. They could have as easily contented themselves with reading, or perhaps merely admiring the illustrations, in Ackermann's tome.

Surprisingly, his only consolation, and he fancied the same was true for one other, was to escape to the outdoors, so new and refreshing was the region to him after years of absence. Usually Kitty was his guide, for she was well informed of the trods thereabout, and was able to lead him on rambles through the beauties of the countryside that took them away from other folk. It was with her that he found himself able to speak his mind on most subjects. The Lakers were foremost in receiving his contempt, contempt she shared with greater reason, for she knew and understood far better than he the beauties they desecrated with their inanities and chatter.

"And did you see that silly Harris woman with her three mirrors today?" he asked as they leaned against a grassy bank. It was the current fashion to "frame" scenic views over one's shoulder.

"Yes, someone should have told her she had chosen the worst time for the fells. She will have a miserably hot walk to get to the station she has chosen. There are no clouds today and the way she goes is little shaded."

"And the mirrors will undoubtedly prove cumbersome. Especially that large oval one. I doubt she can lift it high enough to even glimpse what's over her shoulder."

"She will turn back, I expect," Kitty said comfortably.

"Worse luck for us! I was hoping we'd be rid of her until tea."

"Now, you are very bad to say that," Kitty scolded in a half-hearted fashion. "And besides, there will be others about, you know. At least Mrs. Harris is a known quantity!" she finished with a burst of candor.

"Yes, and we, or rather, you, shan't have to explain it all again. It only took her five or six repetitions to memorize it all. You're the one they bother, for only you have any real knowledge of these parts."

"My father used to take me out on walks around this District. He was an excellent guide and teacher," she explained.

"I wish he were here!" Kit said glumly. "Not that you aren't every bit as good as he, I'm sure."

He didn't notice the quick blush on Kitty's face and the hidden smile. "I'm glad you hold him in esteem."

"I do, and I like him, besides. It would be nice to have another man, a sensible one, that is, to talk to."

"Yes, I can see that that would be a comfort to

you," she answered in a stifled voice, daunted by his bluntness.

Unwittingly, he restored her good feelings with his next words. "The three of us could make these walks together. It would be the greatest thing!"

There was another embarrassed silence. It was gratifying to know that he desired her company even when better was available. But without intending to, Kit had touched on their lack of chaperone. He and Kitty had been encouraged, no, positively ordered to go about alone in a fashion that would never have been tolerated in London. Although he was inexperienced in country ways, he surely must guess from the expression on her mother's face when she saw them off that it was not often done in Cumberland, either. Only the insistence of Mrs. de Fleming and Mrs. Brampton could have overcome the other lady's scruples. Kitty wished that this had not happened, although she welcomed the peace she found in his company and thought that he enjoyed hers, too.

"Tell me once again the name of that peak over yonder! And what are newborn sheep called? Hoggs? Hoggets? And the shearlings and tupps and wethers and wedders and the whole of it?"

She cast him a doubtful smile, wondering if perhaps he *had* sensed her discomfort and was hastening to change the subject. Obligingly, she explained it all again, pointing occasionally to the flock nearby, or to the walls so carefully constructed to allow the sheep to slip through the so-called hogg holes at their base, or toward the summer pastures high on the slopes above them.

Nine

They returned to Broughton Place in time for tea to discover that Mr. Leyburne, despite his absence, had been thinking of them. A note summoning his wife and daughter, and offering a courteous invitation to the de Flemings, had but that moment been delivered to Mrs. Leyburne. Mrs. Brampton was indignant.

"But it was planned that you should stay here for quite another three weeks!"

Mrs. Leyburne forbore to remind her that it was she, Mrs. Brampton, who had so planned. What Mr. Leyburne planned was something entirely different and to be absolutely obeyed by his two ladies, with more than a sense of duty sparking their enthusiasm for leaving the district of Witherslack Woods.

"I fear he speaks to me most particularly on the matter."

"Speaks to you? How can he speak when he isn't here!" The other lady sulked.

"He has written it all down for me to read, you see . . ." She offered the letter to Mrs. Brampton, but that lady ignored it.

"Well, you may not leave for several days in any case. You must be here for the dedication of the little shrine to Sir Thomas Broughton. On that I really must insist!"

Mrs. Leyburne winced and turned back to the note. "I fear that he has been most specific about the arrangement for our returning home. The times are all set out with great particularity. I really could not take it upon myself to overturn his plans."

"Well!" Mrs. Brampton fumed silently, her face saying what her mouth did not. She turned to Mrs. de Fleming. "You and your son shall be staying on, of course!"

Mrs. de Fleming very sensibly did not want to irritate Mrs. Brampton, but she was aware of the fact that it was Kitty Leyburne her son was courting. Such an enterprise is best conducted in person, not over a distance, so she shrugged her shoulders negligently. "It would be only proper to accept such an invitation, considering what plans we have afoot."

Mrs. Leyburne nodded her head. "Yes, my husband is particularly eager that Kit see Leyburne Hall. He feels that a young man should have in his possession all the facts regarding the situation he might well inherit one day."

"What he might inherit from that quarter is little enough. It is what he might inherit from me that counts!"

This angry assertion was greeted by a silent respect it deserved. Although phrased in a vulgar way, there was no denying that it was Mrs. Brampton's money—and ambition—that was the prime mover in encouraging the match between Kit and Kitty. Mrs. de Fleming considered the problem from every angle. One mustn't offend the source of money, of course. But it would do no good to keep Mrs. Brampton's goodwill only to sacrifice Mr. Leyburne's permission for his daughter to wed, a permission still withheld. And there was always the lure of the title to bring Mrs. Brampton to heel.

"Perhaps Kit and I could visit for just a day or two, then bring Kitty back here to the Place," she suggested.

"I am surprised that you should want to visit there at all, considering the neighborhood you should have to enter!" Mrs. Brampton said with spite.

"Whatever can you mean? Surely you do not intend to slight the Leyburnes!" she answered with a smile that attempted to turn it all into a joke.

"The Leyburnes are a most respectable family, and have been so in these parts for generations." Her hostess paused to sneer, then continued. "It is their newest neighbor to whom I refer."

"Whoever can have aroused your disapproval to such a fever?" she was asked with amusement.

"It is not my disapproval that I am concerned with, my dear, but rather yours!"

Mrs. de Fleming bridled, then let the familiarity pass. "Come now, I know of no one in these parts of whom I feel anything less than the utmost respect and regard!" she simpered.

"But I have heard you castigate him myself. Why, only the other day you were telling me of him!"

"Whoever can you mean?" Her mind was racing over the possibilities.

As Mrs. Leyburne knew, there was only one new neighbor. She tried to turn the conversation. "Really, it is nonsense to think that he is so near! We have planned no assemblies or socials that would bring you within proximity of him, it is to be just a private, family gathering. We had thought to show you . . ."

"Who?" Mrs. de Fleming demanded.

"Helm Pele once again has a master in residence!" Mrs. Brampton said triumphantly. "So you see, there is every reason for you to linger here with me. Let Kitty stay on, too. You may return to the Hall as you wish, Mrs. Leyburne."

"That pirate is back in the country?" Mrs. de Fleming gasped.

"Lord Helm has assumed his title and estates," Mrs. Brampton explained.

"He was never proven to be a pirate, Mrs. de Fleming, and you wouldn't have to see him," Mrs. Leyburne said anxiously.

So intent were the ladies on their conversation that they failed to notice the return of Kit and Kitty from their walk. The young couple were just near enough to hear the import of the bickering. The name of Kit's uncle floated in the air, the word pirate had been delivered with loathing, the place Helm Pele mentioned. Kit turned a brick red and taking Kitty's hand, turned her away from the room.

"What is that all about?" she asked with a hiss. "Who is a pirate? Your uncle? Surely not!"

"I shall explain it all later."

Mrs. de Fleming's voice could be heard as she angrily declared that she would not go to within a hundred miles of that monster, no matter what Mr. Leyburne offered in the way of hospitality, or Mrs. Leyburne in promises and assurances. That she and her precious son should be in danger of exposure to such as he was unthinkable. Kit dragged Kitty further away.

"They are talking of going to the Hall, I'll wager," she said, her face eager.

"That may well be," he answered shortly.

"But don't you see, it is our chance to escape! We shall get along much better at the Hall, I assure you. If nothing else, there will be none of these foolish Lakers to tolerate!"

Kit's face brightened for a moment. "That's true." Then he scowled. "But Mama will never go near my uncle. They quarreled long ago, before he had lost all respectability, and she is more than a little afraid of him."

"But why?"

He looked into her inquiring eyes and couldn't bear to explain. "It is our family disgrace, Kitty. It's too shameful."

"Every family has at least one disgrace! What is there to be ashamed of?"

Before she could press him further, Mrs. Leyburne was seen coming out of the drawing room. Her face was flushed and the tears in her eyes showed the degree of agitation she had endured, but her manner was purposefully calm and dignified. "Ah, Kitty, dear, there you are. We must begin packing. Your father has sent for us and arranged our journey home."

"Oh!" Kitty stole a glance at Kit. "And the de Flemings? Will Kit and his mother not come with us?"

Her mother took a deep breath and answered with tolerable composure. "Your father has invited them in terms that are most pressing and hospitable. It was the main reason for him to undertake this trip north, that Kit and his mother should have an opportunity to visit the Hall. But of course Mrs. Brampton would very much like for them to continue here, and I am not sure . . ."

An angry rumble could be heard rolling from the drawing room. The argument had continued between Mrs. de Fleming and Mrs. Brampton, despite the loss of the aggravating presence of the Leyburne spokeswoman.

"Really, this is insufferable, I cannot but believe that you have duped me!" Mrs. de Fleming said as she stalked from the room. The interested audience in the hall tried to appear less interested.

"*I* am not connected with a man of such ill repute, my dear. It was a kindness on my part to refrain from throwing him, and all his nefarious activities, in your face!"

"You knew all along that he was here, didn't you? You lured me to within but a few miles of him, when I have continually sworn to keep my distance from that monster!"

"You have all of Windemere between him and you!" Mrs. Brampton snapped, her tone sarcastic.

"It is not enough! I can never accept the hospitality of someone who has shown herself so insensitive to my express wishes, my very reasonable requirements and expectations." With a swirl of her skirt, she turned to Kit. "Kit, pack up your bags immediately. We are leaving here on the morrow."

"Yes, Mama. But where are we to go?"

"Why, to the Hall, of course! We have traveled north that we might improve our acquaintanceship with the Leyburne family. We shall naturally accept their kind invitation to visit!" And with that total inconsistency announced and made spitefully clear for the benefit of those concerned, she turned to the stairs and mounted them to her room.

Ten

It took Mrs. Leyburne the rest of the day and all her persuasive powers to arrange for a friendly farewell between hostess and guests the following morning. Mrs. de Fleming was all smiles again, Kit and Kitty said everything that was proper, their high spirits on departing put down to youth rather than relief, and Mrs. Brampton only mentioned the forthcoming ceremony they would miss once or twice.

The journey around Windemere into the area between Rydall and Ambleside took them all day to complete, but Mr. Leyburne's preparations were excellent and they found their path smooth and comfortable. Their route was clearly outlined, the inns where they stopped for refreshment ready to serve them, a change of horses where it ought to be. Without saying so aloud, Mrs. Leyburne was pleased to be once again in the excellent care of her husband, rather than Mrs. Brampton, for everything was of the first order with him and nothing left to doubt or chance.

As they lurched over the rough roads in their carriage, Kitty thought of the scene she had witnessed yesterday. If she had heard the ladies rightly, poor Kit had a reprobate and outlaw for an uncle! Lord Helm was apparently well qualified as the black sheep of the de Fleming family, although how he had escaped the justice of the law was beyond her if only half of what had been hinted was true.

But her inherent common sense kept her from carrying her wonder further, for on consideration she knew she had heard the name of Helm before, and in a becoming context. In fact, she rather thought that her father had made a visit to the Pele soon after Lord Helm moved back there, doing so to establish neighborly relations with one living so near. Surely Lord Helm could not precisely be an outlaw if her father were willing to welcome him to the District.

She was not too young to know that often gentlemen had a greater tolerance for the misconduct of other men than could be found among the ladies. Perhaps this was such a case. It was true that an invitation had never been extended to his lordship to visit the Hall, but she was not sure if it was because of her mother's feelings or because the family had soon departed to London, leaving little time for entertaining. She hoped for Kit's sake that the reason was the latter, for it could not be comfortable to have so close a relative held in universal disgust.

She wished she could have discussed the situation further with him, but after the departure of Mrs. de Fleming up the stairs, the group in the hall had broken up, she and Kit to see to packing, her mother to peacemaking. There had been no chance since then for her to be alone with him to express her sympathy, and, frankly, find out more.

Her sympathy was every bit as strong as her curiosity, for she had found herself liking Kit de Fleming more and more. She wished she had been blessed with a brother such as he, for their few explorations into Witherslack Wood had proven more enjoyable than she had expected. She had assumed the role of instructress and guide, and he had not been ashamed of knowing less than she. And Kit had never taken any liberties, such as she had been warned to expect and guard against from a gentleman released from the restraining presence of a chaperone. Far from it, he had behaved in exactly the role she had cast for him, that of considerate brother, and for the first time in her life Kitty found herself at ease in the company of a young man her age. Yes, she had come to like Kit de Fleming very much.

Mrs. de Fleming would have been gratified if she could have known these thoughts were filling Kitty's mind. Instead, she interrupted them.

"The land is grown so much wilder! Surely we have lost our way!" she wailed.

Kitty's mother quickly moved to reassure her. "Not at all, ma'am, not at all. The area we are passing through is well known to us. We are on the right road."

"But the mountains! The heights are quite frightening! They put me in mind of the Alps."

Now it was Kitty's turn to soothe. "They are really not at all so high, Mrs. de Fleming. It is just that everything is so perfectly to scale, that one imagines them to be grander than they really are."

"They look quite grand enough for me! They must be miles high!"

"But, ma'am, Scafell Peak is but some three thousand feet above sea level. I am not very expert at measurements and adding and such, but I think that is less than a mile in distance. Nothing here can be higher than that." She turned to Kit, the only gentleman present and presumably the nearest expert on such mysteries. Since he had as little love for arithmetic and such as she, he did no more than to nod solemnly. His mother was immediately reassured.

"Then it is the pleasantest thing imaginable, to be able to view such grandeur without the inconvenience of great altitudes!" she exclaimed. Kitty, unsure of what inconveniences were experienced at altitudes of miles and miles, merely smiled her agreement and strove to point out some of the beauties for their guests to savor.

"It is well that we are so early in the year, for the heather and bracken have not cloaked the fells and pikes," she said after a while.

"Surely you cannot dislike the beauty such vegetation brings," Mrs. de Fleming protested with a smile to show the girl she knew she was only joking. "Greenery is so refreshing, so beautiful! It can only be admired."

"But yes, I *can* dislike it! They cover the rocky grandeur of the landscape and turn it soft and gentle! One cannot but begrudge the loss of the splendor they conceal, however much one enjoys them on other ground."

"Rocky grandeur? Splendor?" Mrs. de Fleming savored the words. While staying at Broughton Place she had ventured forth only rarely, and then always in a carriage. This was all very new to her. "Yes, my dear, I begin to see your point. We must aim for a sublime experience, not merely a pretty one! Everyone says so. Rocky grandeur? Indeed! The very thing."

Kit and Kitty exchanged disconcerted glances. They had thought to escape the Lakers. Indeed! They were taking one with them. Suppressing a desire to giggle, Kitty turned Mrs. de Fleming's attention to an interesting arrangement of stones, and the subject passed off. Kit, lurching against the rough jolting of the carriage's passage, recalled an obligation with a guilty start. Yes, he must remember to dash off a note to Lady Madge. She would be wondering what had become of him.

Eleven

They had soon reestablished the habit of taking long rambles across the countryside around Leyburne Hall. As before, Kitty assumed the role of guide and teacher, Kit that of pupil, and they rubbed along together famously.

"Isn't it beyond belief that it could all be so beautiful?" Kit asked her one morning as they watched some storm clouds hover over a rugged peak. "It is like entering another world. London seems very far away."

"I suppose it is far away, in ways that mere miles can't measure," she rejoined. "It is all very simple and quiet here, not at all like town. No balls, no assemblies, no carriage drives in the Park. One forgets about fashion."

"Carriage drives in the Park?" he laughed. "There are no carriage drives at all. At least not where we have come today." They had taken a particularly rough route over rocks and gullies and twisted brush. No fashionable phaeton or brougham could have hoped to make its way through such obstacles. The two young people had barely managed to make their way on foot.

"*No* carriage drives," she agreed with a smile, glancing down at her torn skirt and scratched hands. Modish costume would not have survived any better than stylish transport. It was as well she had worn an old and faded muslin, as usual. "I should have brought some gloves to wear," she murmured as she stretched out her battered hands.

"Not at all, do as you please. Unless you have hurt yourself?"

"Oh, no, just gathered considerable dirt." She paused for a moment, then harkened back to something he had said. "That is the biggest difference of all, between here and there! One may do as one pleases in the country. There is no fear of offending polite scruples, only of offending one's own. It is so tiresome always to be heeding such false precepts of conduct one finds in London."

He thought this over for a moment, then nodded his head in agreement. "A certain time to stroll up Bond Street, a certain hat or cravat or waistcoat one must wear, the right clubs to belong to, the right parties to attend, even one's vices decided for one on the basis of fashion!"

"Surely not!"

"But yes! It is entirely honorable to gamble away vast sums of money. It is expected of one! Only one must always pay up. Now, if one is faced with trifling tradesmen's bills, one may ignore them, that is counted no shame." He was enjoying the argument now. "And many of my friends indulge in foolish escapades that would cause their arrest if it weren't for their influence and money. Silly things, like fighting with Charlies or tipping over someone's carriage, or putting out all the lights on a street."

She was giggling and offered one protest. "These latter sound more like escapades than vice! Your friends are too high-spirited!"

"Yes, you are right, but it is wrong that there is no natural outlet for their energies. No way for them to spend their enthusiasm in a productive fashion. Instead, they waste themselves on petty amusements that tend toward the vicious."

"I will agree that to gamble so extravagantly is not right," she murmured.

He began to protest that there was more done than mere gambling, then stopped himself with surprise. Surely he should not be discussing such things with a young lady? How could he have so forgotten himself! He hastily tried to brush aside his own arguments.

"Such pastimes, whether petty activities that waste time or full-fledged vice, seem worse than pointless in the midst of all this grandeur. How can one worry about the proper arrangement of one's cravat when one feels so close to nature?"

"To God?" she said in the same instant.

They were embarrassed by this intrusion of the profound in their light-hearted talk, and for a moment could find nothing to say.

"Yes, one is close to God, to nature, and all of it out here. I'm beginning to find my own roots, too, you know, for I was born hereabouts, and all my father's family was from this District. I am learning things I had long since forgotten, things about the countryside and about myself."

Kitty, seeing an opening for the questions she had longed to put to him, opened her mouth to speak, but he forestalled her. "What is that structure over there?" he asked, pointing down a deep little valley on their right.

Glancing in the direction he indicated, she said with a shrug, "It's but a mine."

"A mine? I did not know that there was such an abundance of precious metals here about."

"There isn't, not now. At least it isn't worthwhile to bring it to the surface. It wasn't always so. Wad was used for munitions making and the mine over near Seathwaite was reckoned the only source of high-grade wad in the world."

"Wad? I am learning more than a new landscape. All the language is strange to me, too."

"Wad, plumbago, graphite. They are all the same. As little as twenty years ago the big mine yielded tons and tons. Now the pencil factory in Kendal doesn't even buy the stuff, so no one brings it up."

"It sounds a commonplace sort of venture in any case," he said with a nod toward the right.

"Commonplace? The wad was so valuable that special laws were passed to keep it from being pirated and smuggled! There were glorious battles fought to keep the mineral in the hands of its rightful owners, with armed men guarding the mine and the pack trains carrying it out of the District. My papa has told me that you can always identify the smugglers' pack trains. Instead of placing bells on the ponies' harnesses, they left them off and what is more, muffled their hooves with straw so that they would make no sound!"

"You sound very bloodthirsty," he mocked. "Smugglers and battles and armed guards."

"No, I do not regret that the battles are no more, although they must have been stirring affairs. But much wealth was brought into the District by the mines. Now most are abandoned."

"Most? Surely I have heard of other mining ventures in the area?"

"Oh, there is much copper to be found about Coniston and Paddy Ends. There are many great enterprises still, and there are many small miners who are still feathering for what they can find. They say the bloomies have caused so many trees to be downed near the mines that the landscape is desolate, and that's no good thing."

He was laughing all the while, at her feathering, her bloomies, and her air of casual interest in all this that was so new to him. Pleased with his enjoyment, she took the opportunity to direct their talk into other more personal channels. Anything, good or bad, that was near to Kit's heart excited the greatest interest in her.

"They say that there is a goodly deposit of copper still being worked near Helm Pele. Do you know anything of it?"

Instantly he was rigid. "No, I cannot. I thought I had explained that."

"Yes, you had, and it is really quite bad of me to still be curious, but I am. It is not that I'm seeking sensation, I just don't understand it all. Forgive me for being pert."

"You aren't pert." Kit mulled over her obvious desire for information, admitted with such disarming frankness. He was aware that a natural confusion must have arisen from her observation of his mother's contradictory conduct; and her air of sympathy, which he had come to like and trust, reassured him. He had never discussed this with anyone but Mrs. de Fleming, and even with that person there had been little discussion, mostly lecture and invective. For the first time he had come to feel that *he* had a friend and confidant he could turn to for comfort and counsel.

"It is just that my uncle was guilty of terrible crimes. You know that the family's lesser title is Scandale? They called him Lord Scandal."

"Then why hasn't he been arrested and imprisoned?"

"It is not as easy as that, at least I don't quite understand it all myself."

"Tell me about it." She had turned her face to his, her head resting on her two hands, her elbows firmly embedded in the young heather. She had commanded him to tell her the tale, and to his surprise, Kit did just that.

"He was in some sort of disgrace here at home, and his family sent him off to the West Indies until the controversy should die down and he could return. Some friends or other had property out there and a place was found for Uncle Matthew." He was talking eagerly now, but with a storyteller's unconscious desire to stir suspense, he paused to see how she was taking this part of the tale.

"What had he done?"

"No one knows, or if they do, they aren't telling me."

"Do you mean that they never let him come back?" she asked with disappointment. "If they can't even remember what it was he did, that doesn't seem fair."

"No, it's not for that reason he was banished, all but disinherited. Something worse happened."

Another pause.

"Well, what? Tell me!"

"He became involved with some unruly types out there and fell into really bad company."

"All young men do that, or so my mother says. She says they outgrow it."

"Well, before he had a chance to do so, Uncle Matthew had become a pirate!"

"Pirate?" She thought for a moment, memories of tales of horror fresh in her mind. "Oh, no! You mean like Black Beard and all the rest?"

"That's it exactly. So now you see why he is so hated by my mother. It is only the entailment that gives him the title. She says that if my great-grandfather could have arranged it otherwise, he would have settled everything on Papa."

"Oh, my! That is a dreadful scandal to have in one's family. Quite the worst I have ever heard!" She stared at him with considerable respect and he accepted her awe with good grace.

"He only just recently came back to claim the title and all," he explained airly. "It was the most frightful shock to poor Mama—she positively loathes him."

"I wonder that he wasn't arrested and put into

chains the instant he set foot on English soil!" she protested staunchly.

"Well, the West Indies is a long way off, you see, and I imagine that evidence is hard to come by at so great a distance. But there is one final proof of his ill deeds!"

She leaned closer, her imagination racing over the possibilities. What could it be? A peg leg? A patch over his eye? A hook in place of a lost hand, green parrots sitting on either shoulder, nautical language, ruffian companions???

"He has come back loaded with gold!"

"No-o-o! Pieces of eight?"

"Something like that. He is very rich in any case."

"All that ill-gotten profit, and he hasn't been punished for any of what he did!" So great was her indignation that she had scrambled to her feet and balanced with hands on hips.

Kit shook his head sadly. "And he probably never will be!"

So great was the impression made on her by Kit's story and his sincere belief in the whole of it, that Kitty forgot her earlier uncertainties of the reputation of Lord Helm. Although she could not suppose that her father was capable of tolerating piracy, bloodshed, stealing, and murder, for no gentleman, no matter how liberal he might be, could be *that* tolerant, she failed to question his judgement. Instead, she merely forgot it.

On returning to the Hall, even the details of Kit's story were driven from her mind by an event that enabled her to cling to only the most important of the secrets he had imparted, namely that his uncle, the present Lord Helm, was a pirate!

What could have so emptied her head of romantic notions and feminine sympathy for her friend? It would seem that Mrs. Leyburne had done her job as a peacemaker all too well. That afternoon, unannounced and uninvited, there had come to the Hall Mrs. Brampton, with maid, carriage, tales of the consecration of the shrine, and the greatest will in the world to manage them all to suit herself. Their peace was at an end. Courtship was to begin in earnest.

Unbeknownst to the inhabitants of Leyburne Hall, there was yet another new arrival in the District, one anxiously concerned with the progress of that courtship and ready to interfere as soon as she could. In fact, this individual was about to create for herself such an opportunity.

Twelve

The whiff of perfume, its fragrance almost forgotten, assailed Kit's nostrils as he turned the letter over in his hands. With the smell came a flood of memories, dear, happy memories, that had somehow begun to blur. It had taken him nearly an hour to find this moment of solitude after the letter had been delivered; it had arrived in full view of the household. Only chance had given him the task of distributing the contents of the mail pouch, enabling him to slip the missive addressed to himself into his trouser pocket.

The thick blob of wax sealing the paper shattered under his thumb and he unfolded the heavy sheet of paper. As he began to read he was thunderstruck to see that the message was superseded by a Grassmere address. He had failed to notice the absence of a frank or postage on the exterior of the letter.

What could have brought Lady Madge so near? All the way north to Cumberland? She was but a few miles from the Hall, from his mother, from the Leyburne family who were extending to him their hospitality in the hope he would marry their daughter. What wild whimsy or impulse had inspired her to leave London, had propelled her along the roads north to the Lake District? What madness . . . ?

He forced himself to read further, attending to the ornate script with some care in an effort to decipher the meaning of her words. After some moments the words, their spelling and intent, were altogether too clear.

"Cheri,—I cannot bear to be parted from you for so long! To see your dear face, hear your sweet voice, it is all I have dreamed of, all I have longed for, since you left London that dreadful Wednesday morning . . ."

Kit shook himself with momentary irritation. He had left on a Tuesday, of that he was sure.

"The cloudburst that marred that day was nothing to the tears I shed! London has been a desert without you, a veritable Sahara without your dear presence! Your precious letters have been treasured next to my heart . . ."

Kit could not help but squirm. There had been only the one letter he had sent off to London, written the very morning after his arrival here at the Hall.

". . . but I would rather you were here."

And once he had longed to be there!

"I am at Grassmere, as you can see from the direction I noted at the beginning of my little note, with my kind, dear friends Mr. and Mrs. Sopthwaite. He has something to do with making pencils, but despite this close association with Trade, and that of a lowly nature, he and his wife have souls of the greatest sublimnity! I traveled north with them, arriving but yesterday."

Sopthwaite? Kit recalled no such name amongst the hosts of Lady Madge's friends and admirers.

"They have rented a cottage, just a stop from Grassmere itself. Darling, the wonder of it, the beauty! The shattering impact of such a profound experience, for as much as a glimpse of the Lake is that! and to enjoy it daily! It is such that you cannot appreciate unless you have had the opportunity yourself, and such is our fortune every day, every hour of the day. On waking one has but to walk a few yards from the door to see the sweetest view imaginable! There are just a select few of us visiting here, and we are all people of the highest sensibilities, the purest vision, the deepest emotions! In short, there is nothing to intrude on the rapture, nothing that is in the slightest degree untasteful or vulgar.

"But I prattle on of nothings. When the opportunity to be near you was offered, I seized it! Dearest, I could not bear the separation for another day longer! Surely you, who love as I do, will understand the depths of pain that drove me north. Your heart will sing as does mine that we are but a few miles from one another! I'm sure you must have sensed my nearness these past few hours, *n'est-ce pas?*

"Kit, darling boy, I must see you soon. Immediately! My heart can wait not another hour, not even a minute. It cannot bear it! I shall be waiting for you at the station on Grassmere that gives one a view of the greatest isolation and grandeur of the water. Surely you know the one of which I speak? One can see a tumbled-down cottage from there. It is even by a little shelter. (They call it a bield in these parts, is that not quaint? It so adds to the richness of the aesthetic experience when one encounters these little novelties!) I shall be there on the morrow, at the hour before noon. Do not fail me! I bear the most urgent news, news of momentous importance to the two of us and our life together in the years ahead. I cannot bear to think of the hours that must pass before I shall have your strong arms about me, feel your soft lips on mine! Being separated from you is such torture! I cannot write more.

"Darling, until tomorrow,

"Your adoring Madge.

"PostScriptum,—Darling, don't forget to bring your mirror. This station is said to give one a sublime visual experience. How romantic, the two of us sharing such sublime joy together! Two souls twined as one! Madge."

Bring a mirror? Had she gone mad? And as for the much vaunted station she had designated for their rendezvous, Kit suspected that it was valued for its easy access. Too many of the Lakers were like their forerunner Thomas Grey, afraid of the imagined dangers of the District and far too timid to face the fells and meres on their own rugged terms.

What was he to do? He couldn't ignore the letter and the meeting it proposed, foolish as the suggestion was. Lady Madge had been very, well, very kind to him. What was he saying? Kind? She had loved him! She still did. Her letter breathed that in every word, every line. She had been driven by this love to seek him out, no matter what the risk to her reputation, no matter what the danger of scandal. He must find some way of meeting her at the appointed time and place. He owed her that much. And besides, if he failed her, she might do something really disastrous, like come to the Hall!

It should be easy enough. By now he knew the area around Grassmere like the palm of his hand. Long treks with Kitty had seen to that. The station Lady Madge had chosen was but a half hour's walk from where he now stood, and it had the advantage of some degree of isolation. No one need know of the rendezvous.

But what excuse could he have for scrambling off alone? Kitty, so kind and dear, would never question him. But his mother? Her mother? Mrs. Brampton? He shuddered at the thought of their inquisition, the arch, prying questions directed to him, the teasing insinuations, all followed by his mother's direct command that he tell all.

He must think of something. He must see Lady Madge—in all kindness she had a right to expect that of him. Honor demanded it. He would try to break his news to her as gently as he could.

For he saw it all now. He had never really loved her. It had been merely a foolish infatuation, a school-boy crush! He could see that clearly enough.

He was well beyond such callow behavior. He had grown, matured. His trip back to his own part of the world, where he had been born and bred, where his family had made their home for generations, had brought him to a truer understanding of himself. He belonged here, in Cumberland, not in London with its frivolous distractions, and empty, soul-killing pastimes. He did not belong with Lady Madge; that would never do, for Lady Madge was the quintessence of London and all it stood for.

Not that he would never go back to the metropolis again. He would one day have to assume his seat in the House of Lords, that was clear, and assume the burdens of political responsibility which he would inherit. But his heart would dwell among the fells and meres.

With this uplifting resolve made, he returned his attention to the letter. He would just have to slip away somehow. Perhaps Kitty would help with that?

No, not that! Never! To drag her in, all innocent, to ask her to participate in something shabby? The thought was abhorrent.

Perhaps . . .

"Kit, where have you taken yourself off to?" His mother's voice carried across the lawn and through the topiary of the garden, breaking his revery.

"Here, Mama. Here, by the statue of Pan." He stuffed the letter back into his pocket and hurried to the turn in the path to meet her.

"Ah, yes, there you are, you naughty boy. We have been looking all over for you! You must hear of the most delightful scheme which is afoot. Between us, Mrs. Leyburne and I have come up with an exciting scheme! So clever of us! I have come to ask you your opinion of it."

"Yes, Mama."

"Tomorrow we shall all set out on an expedition! Isn't that a delightful prospect?"

"Mama!"

"You two young people will show your elders the views that you have so selfishly been keeping to yourselves. You shall be our guides! La, won't that be grand?"

"But . . . !"

"Never fear, we shall travel in comfort. I hear that much of the way can only be traveled on foot—that seems to be the custom hereabouts, not like the dear lovely glade of Mrs. Brampton's wood to the south—but that cannot be helped. And we will make it as civilized as we can, that goes without saying. There will be hampers of food, and chairs and blankets. It is to be a picnic, you see! The servants will be sent out ahead in the morning. Mrs. Leyburne is seeing to it all now!"

Kit struggled for composure, a new emotion rising in his breast. "It would seem that there is little I can do to advise you, Mama. You have everything well in hand, as you always do."

"The details of the food and drink are really to be left to Mrs. Leyburne, of course. She is our hostess and that is only proper. Although I did just drop a hint or two. But we have not settled on our destination for tomorrow. What shall be our goal for this little outing? There seem to be too many objects of interest rather than too few, an embarrassment of things to do and see. Miss Kitty suggested that I consult with you. What station would you suggest we visit? What would be the most inspiring view?"

Kit's mind spun for a moment or two. What was he to do? To say? What *could* he do? He knew his mother too well to hope that he could withdraw himself from the picnic.

There was a lovely prospect from a station but a half mile from his appointed rendezvous with Lady Madge. It would please his mother and the other ladies, he was sure. He could slip away and spare a few moments with Madge. True, that half mile was a steep, rocky one, almost over the back of a pike. It would be a difficult climb. But he must see her, somehow. Honor demanded it!

"Well, what shall it be, dear boy? Grassmere? Chapel Stile? Rydall Water? How seriously you ponder them all! Such a dear son I have, to have such a care for his mama's amusement!"

"Grassmere it shall be, Mama. We must be sure that you have an opportunity to see Grassmere. You do so admire Mr. Wordsworth's work and he is said to have found all his inspiration for poetry when walking along the shores of Grassmere."

"Surely that is more distant than Rydall Water?" she protested doubtfully.

"But we shall be able to travel much of the way by carriage, Mama. Only the last quarter mile or less must be covered on foot, a mere stroll for the ladies."

She turned this over in her mind, then smiled. Kit was never to know if it was the prospect of traveling most of the distance in a vehicle, or his reminder of the ever popular and admired William Wordsworth that swayed her.

"Grassmere! The very thing. You have thought of everything, darling Kit. La! How clever of you to remember your poor old mother's comfort and amusement!"

"It is the very least I can do."

Thirteen

The fells were at their most magnificent. Slatey colors on the peaks merged into the deep plum of crevices, the still-barren rock face revealing its rugged grandeur unsoftened by the layer of heather that would blur it in a month. Every chimney, every force, every pike and interesting rocky outcrop were all there to be savored. Even the weather was assisting the scene, for picturesque clouds were scooting across the sky, marking the backdrop with strange shapes and contortions. The summits were lost in low-lying cloud from time to time.

Mist enshrouded Mrs. de Fleming's new hat, beading it with droplets of water. A cloud had descended to engulf their hillside path.

"Are you quite sure we shouldn't postpone the expedition to another day? The weather is so lowering!" she complained for the fifth time. She reckoned without taking the spirit of the true natives into account.

"No, no, the clouds will make it all perfection!" Mrs. Brampton enthused.

"Yes, but of course! They add infinitely to the grandeur of the fells. Just look there. See how the black of the cloud shows off the gray of the peak?" This from Mrs. Leyburne.

"Besides, everyone else is out," Kit added with gentle irony. His mother was sounding like the typical Laker, and he couldn't help but squirm for her conduct.

What he had said was true. They could see flashes of reflecting light whenever the occasional ray of sunlight struck a mirror. At times the surrounding slopes seemed to be atwinkle with small pinpricks of light.

"But what if it rains? We shall be drenched!" his mother wailed. "If we were to turn back now . . ."

"A brisk walk will keep us warm," Mrs. Brampton assured her. She was sensibly dressed in stout boots, her oldest; and dress and pelisse, with a cloak packed in one of the wicker baskets a servant was carrying. Her hat was a sturdy felt one that would shed water.

"I don't think we need worry about it raining, Mrs. de Fleming," Mrs. Leyburne added with more kindness, one eye on the muslin and lace concoction her guest was wearing. "We may be a trifle damp from this cloud, but Mungo assured me this morning that there would be no rain, or so say his joints. There are invariably correct in predicting the weather, I assure you."

"Besides, the heat would be dreadful if the sun were shining," Mrs. Brampton proclaimed before moving out ahead of the group.

"And there would be such a haze raised if it were warm!" agreed Mrs. Leyburne. "It would quite obscure the view." Beyond inducing a grim silence, these assurances had little of their intended effect on their object.

His mother's talk of soakings and damp stirred a new hope in Kit's breast. Perhaps Lady Madge, that most delicate of urban creatures, would be daunted by the ill appearance of the day. She might not arrive at their meeting place after all. The more he toyed with this idea, the more likely it seemed. Lady Madge, who never went anywhere on foot while in London, would surely shrink from a walk of one and a half miles in weather threatening rain. She would put off their rendezvous. His fears were all a meaningless pother.

"Do look at that man with a pack pony over yonder!" Kitty said unexpectedly. Of all the company, she was the only one who was truly noticing their surroundings. She was pointing in the direction she meant and Kit looked up to see a picturesque native, a man dressed in a working-man's smock, leading a small pony across a steep trod. The sound of the animal's many bells tinkled across the valley.

"An honest man, it would seem. He is announcing his comings and goings with ringing peals," Kit joked. "No straw to muffle the hooves of that beast."

"Alas, no smuggler, either!" Kitty said with a giggle.

"Ponies? Do you mean to tell me there is some way of getting up to this shelter without walking? I had not heard of these ponies before," Mrs. de Fleming snapped, a pout marring the line of her mouth. "I would be much more comfortable riding, I am sure."

"On, no, my dear, you would not. Only the very young or the very vulgar resort to such a device," Mrs. Brampton objected. The other lady turned to stare at her sullenly.

"And your ride would be far from comfortable," Mrs. Leyburne quickly interjected. "The little animals lurch in a most alarming fashion. I once tried to ride one, oh, many years ago, and I was in constant dread of a tumble. It even causes one's stomach to feel unsettled, as if one were riding a ship in rough weather."

"We are but a few minutes from the sight Kit has chosen for our picnic, ma'am," Kitty soothed. "There will be a lovely place to sit and rest while the food is being taken out of the hampers. And there is even an overhanging ledge to provide you with shelter if there should happen to be a shower."

Fortunately Kitty's words were truer than she realized, for around the next bend in the trod they could just see the small clearing that was their objective. Mrs. de Fleming, seeing the protective shelf for herself, straightened her hat, turned her back to the rest of the company, and marched forward with a better humor.

The servants had arrived nearly an hour before, and the company found that blankets and cushions were awaiting them, all neatly arranged and inviting. With a sigh, Mrs. de Fleming sank into a well-cushioned niche, leaving the responsibility of overseeing the unpacking of the hampers to the other ladies. She was seemingly oblivious to the wonders all around her, to her companions, even to the weather, for she had leaned back with her eyes closed and made no sound or gesture. Kit, seeing her thus, made to seize the opportunity and began to amble off further down the path. He reckoned that he would have to go some several hundred yards before he would reach a point suitable to scrambling over the pike to the rendezvous on the other side.

"Kit?"

He continued walking, pretending he hadn't heard.

"Kit!"

It was impossible to ignore his mother's voice this time, for everyone had turned to see what was afoot.

"Yes, Mama?"

"Surely you do not intend to wander off alone? Such a hankering for solitude is hardly in the spirit of our little outing." She now had both eyes open and was even sitting up, the better to observe his reactions and enforce her authority.

"I had just wanted to explore a little way along the path, before we eat, the walk would stimulate my appetite . . ."

"Fine. But I am sure Katherine would wish to accompany you."

"But . . ."

"It would be courteous of you to ask."

By now everyone, including and especially Katherine, were pretending to ignore the dialogue.

Kitty's face was averted over a particularly deep hamper.

Kit was trapped. He hadn't intended to involve anyone else in this meeting, especially not Kitty. Now he was faced with either confiding in another or somehow hoodwinking someone he considered his friend. Then Kitty came to his rescue.

"I had intended to help my mama here, Mrs. de Fleming. Let Kit go off and explore on his own. He may find another path for us to take after lunch; wouldn't that be an adventure?"

"Nonsense. You shall go with him, my dear. There are plenty of hands about here to do the work. Run along with Kit, now," Mrs. Brampton commanded her.

Seeing that there was to be no remedy for the situation, Kit turned to Kitty and held out his hand to her. "Yes, it will be far more jolly to have someone with me. Do come."

Seeing that he was smiling, she ended her hesitation and took his hand. "If you would really like it."

"There is no one I would rather explore the fells with than you, as you are well aware." He could say this with sincerity, for as far as it went, it was the truth. But if only he could have chosen another time for their joint venture!

Aware that the appointed time was fast approaching, he turned to the path, setting a brisk pace, his mind turning over excuses and apologies.

It was easier than he had thought to leave Kitty behind. They came to a chimney cutting into the rocks, one with inviting holds and likely grasping points for pulling oneself up. What could be more natural than for Kit to want to investigate it? It was almost exactly where he calculated he should cross the pike. There was even a patch of moss that Kitty could sit on in some degree of comfort while she waited.

"You don't mind being deserted like this? I shall be away only for a few brief moments, I assure you."

"Not at all, Kit. You go off and explore. This is what you were intending all along, wasn't it? I shall wait here in perfect comfort until you return, enjoying the view and avoiding the work of unpacking the hampers."

He knew that to some extent she was putting forward a brave front, for she never minded being helpful when the occasion offered, but he smiled his appreciation. She was the kindest person, always making things easier for other people! And the prospect from this point on the path was unusually picturesque. It would not all be dull for her while she awaited his return.

"If you're sure."

"Of course I am. And not a word to the others that you found your solitude after all."

"Then I leave you to a sublime view, Kitty," he joked. "It is far more than merely pretty!"

"If only I had thought to bring my mirror!"

"You go too far!"

They laughed for a moment, then she added, "I shall be able to go back and enthuse to the others, and even insist that they come and inspect it!"

"It would be more than they deserve."

"Perhaps. But Kit, do have a care! It is a steep climb you undertake."

"Of course. I shan't fall."

"And not just that. It may not be raining today, but the mist does seem to be thickening. Just look at the peak over there. It is only now being submerged in clouds."

"Yes, well, of course . . ." he began impatiently.

"You will have a difficult time of it if you can't see where to put your hands and feet," she said point-blank, but with a smile.

A trifle sheepish, he smiled back. "You know far more about it than I do, Kitty. You are right. Thank you for the warning. I shall have a care."

Fourteen

Kitty sat down on her mossy stone with a rueful grin on her face. Well, Kit had certainly gotten his solitary walk, she thought to herself. And there she sat, her dress soiled at the hem after an unexpected slip, even a tear showing in the skirt from where the bushes had clung too tenaciously while they had pushed their way through. Her hands were soiled and grubby from the times she had had to push back branches and vines to keep herself from becoming hopelessly entrapped. If Mrs. de Fleming imagined she had sent her son off on a romantic stroll with the heiress, she was sadly mistaken.

Kitty tried to make what repairs she could, but without water or any sort of washcloth larger than her handkerchief, she could effect little improvement. If only she had known it, her windblown curls and flushed cheeks made her far more attractive than usual, remarkably so. But all she was aware of were the stains of her journey up the path.

At least the view was rather nice. The sun had somehow contrived to edge the higher clouds with silver, even gold showed in spots, and thus gilded, the gray masses blew across the sky, allowing occasional glimpses of blue as if to reward the watchers below. Mrs. Brampton had been right, clouds added infinitely to the grandeur of the scene. Kitty hoped Mrs. de Fleming was enjoying it all.

In the valley below she could just glimpse the trod that the pony and its driver had taken. The path smoothed out to a wide, comfortable way once down the valley floor, for there it escaped the pitch of the fell. The valley was dotted with sheep, moving slowly up the hill as they cropped the grass, occasionally breaking through the hogg holes in the stone walls to forage farther afield. The walls themselves darkly delineated the various heafs. A drift road wended its way up from a stone and slate farmstead to the pasture above. Soon the shepherds would be moving up to their saeters high in the mountains, from there to tend their flocks during the summer. Those mountains were already beginning to show the softening effect brought on by their summer vegetation.

It was a pity she was not just a few yards further along the path, if there was indeed more to it beyond the pile of rubble that blocked her view and her way. She thought she might be able to see the waterfall of the force on the far side of the valley. She was sure that the direction Kit had taken would lead him onto a path that would do just that from a tumbled-down bield. She regretted that they hadn't made that their objective for the day. Her curiosity piqued, she began considering ways and means of achieving her view. Soon she was crawling over the pile of small stones and dirt that barred her way.

There *was* more of the path, such that she dimly remembered from jaunts in summers past. It seemed to be wider and better trod than her recollection had led her to expect, and Kitty guessed that the various visitors to the District had discovered a new station from which to declaim and exclaim over the beauties of nature. And as she had guessed, one of those included the beck, now in full spate after last night's rains, pouring down the hillside to create a magnificent force. For a moment she forgot that she had done her appearance little good in her efforts to reach her present position, and contented herself with admiring the waterfall.

Then the crackle and rustling of disturbed underbrush caused her to heed where she was, and in what condition. If she was right in her surmises, she was being approached by one or more of the Lakers; she could conceive of no business that would bring a native there. With a glance down at her bedraggled gown, she turned back to the rockslide, determined to escape. It would never do to be caught out by strangers in her present state! And she had little use for them in any case.

Unfortunately, the slide was still sliding. Every time she thought she had found a foothold that would carry her over the top of the rubble, it fell away from under her. More loose stones and dirt were providing the raw materials that kept the pile of rocks from diminishing, and she was faced with what seemed to be an insurmountable barrier. Then the Laker was upon her.

"Well, well, what have we here? A country girl out for a stroll?" The voice was a deep one, that of a man, and turning around, Kitty saw that he was alone. Another glance caused her heart to stop, for there, standing before her with his hands on his hips, was a cavalry officer in uniform, a uniform of *her* officer's regiment. The blond hair, the pale blue eyes, the breadth of his shoulders, all conspired to confuse her for a moment. Had he come to find her? Had he not given her up after all?

"Can't you say anything, little maid? A pretty little thing like you must surely know how to talk. You must carry on with all the lads hereabout, eh?"

Whoever he was, he was not her cavalier. He didn't even seem to know her. In fact, and this was the most embarrassing aspect of the situation for her, he seemed to have taken Kitty for some lowly serving maid, or a laborer's daughter. At least that was her guess. Surely a gentleman would never speak to a lady in such a familiar, even vulgar tone of voice.

"As we have not been introduced, it would hardly be fitting for me to acknowledge your greetings, sir!" she said as stiffly as she could while trying one more time to make her way over the slide. Unfortunately, slipping down on one's knees instead of making a dignified exit does not impress anyone, not even the lady herself.

"On your feet." He grabbed each of her arms above the elbows and pulled her up.

"You may release me this instant, sir!" she protested when one of his hands lingered. She was answered by a squeeze and found herself being drawn closer to the man.

"Let me go!"

"You can talk! I knew it." He tried to slip his arm around her waist, but she managed to wriggle away from him. Unfortunately, he stood between her and the clear end of the path, her only easy way of escape. There was nothing to do but turn to the slide once again and struggle over it if she could.

This time she had managed to pull herself halfway up its side, a helpful branch almost in reach, when the officer once again took action. A kick of his boot knocked the earth out from under her yet again, and she landed in a tumble at his feet. He threw back his head and roared with laughter.

Now Kitty was angry, truly angry. "How dare you! How dare you!" She was so infuriated that she could only keep repeating this phrase as she pulled herself to her feet, avoiding the man as best she could. Never in her life had she been treated in such a rude, disrespectful manner, and nothing had taught her how to deal with it. In her present state of indignation, even her native wit had deserted her.

"You will stand aside and let me pass!" she ordered.

"So, you're going to try the other direction, eh?

Just what are you about? You *were* all too anxious to reach the other side of that rubble. Now, what could be so appealing over there? Is it a trysting place?"

Ignoring him, Kitty tried to slip past him again, for no other alternative seemed available. With another gargantuan laugh, he swept her under one arm and squeezed her tight.

"No, no, you shan't, wench. You're too pretty to let run away. I'll just keep ahold o' you."

Kitty had begun to scream, but a rough hand covered her mouth and she was being dragged back to the slide. A wiff of spirit-ladened breath reached her nostrils and she fought all the harder.

"We'll just investigate the other side of this blockage here, my sweet heart, just the two of us alone. Won't that be nice?" And with surprising ease he heaved the two of them, Kitty firmly tucked under one arm, to the top of the treacherous heap of rocks and stones. From there, breathless but triumphant, he was able to observe the other side.

"A pretty little glade, love. Of course, the view isn't as spectacular, as on this side you miss the waterfall. The ladies would rate it only pretty, I venture. But it will do well enough for us. No one will think to climb over this roadblock. We'll be left well alone here."

He continued to ignore Kitty's struggles as he inspected the little clearing with full approval. But suddenly, her efforts had more than their desired effect, for once again, the ground gave way beneath him and they both slid down the little hill, landing in a tangle at its foot.

"Back where we started, eh?" he laughed jovially. Kitty continued to kick and scratch, even bit one of his hands that was too temptingly near.

"You're a saucy one. I like that. Well, if it's this side that pleases you after all, so be it!"

He hauled them both to their feet, keeping one hand on Kitty's wrist. Despite her twisting and kicking, he managed to grab her by each shoulder and pull her to him.

"My father will punish you for this! How dare you treat me in such a way? You will be taken before the magistrate and . . ."

His laughter drowned her words. "Arrested for trifling with some serving wench who's no better than she ought to be? Don't be daft, girl. A little chit like you must learn to accept life's little surprises, especially if you go wandering off alone in these damned mountains. Besides, you know you don't mind, do you? Don't make such a fuss of it!"

This time he had succeeded in slipping his arm around her waist, and Kitty found herself crushed against his chest. The wave of alcoholic breath that reached her nearly caused her to faint, but then, to her horror, his face was near hers and she was twisting and turning to avoid his punishing mouth, but to no avail.

Fifteen

The chimney and pike had proven even more formidable than Kit had expected, but he made good time despite these obstacles and felt a surge of triumph as he landed on his feet near the appointed meeting place.

There was an expression of shocked surprise on Lady Madge's face as she watched Kit tumbling down the slope.

"Kit, dearest, whatever have you done? Why did you choose such a precipitous route? What an odd quirk! And just look at you!" She had taken a step back.

"Good grief, Lady Madge, have you any idea how difficult it was for me to get away? This isn't London, you know!"

She was unimpressed. "But, still, surely the path would have been the easier route to take.

And one that would have left you in some degree respectable as to your attire. You look like a rag picker!"

"Easier route? Rag picker? My mother, and Mrs. Leyburne, and Mrs. Brampton, not to mention Kitty, are all on the other side of this pike, having a picnic. There was no way I could avoid accompanying them today, hence I made the best of a bad situation. You gave me little leeway, after all. It was a miracle that I was able to get here at all! Of all the ridiculous starts . . . !"

Her expression changed and she interrupted him ruthlessly. "My dear, brave Kit! Climbing over those dangerous mountains just to meet with his poor lady love! Such courage! Such daring! Here, you must sit down here, where you will be comfortable. You might have done yourself some injury! Are you sure you are all right? You haven't hurt yourself? Do tell me the truth, darling, no courteous evasions! I should never forgive myself if something happened to you because of me!"

Courteous evasions were the furthest things from Kit's mind.

"Dash it all, Madge, I'm fine, just fine!" he grumbled.

"I know you had told me so, but please, you must exercise only the greatest candor with me! Common civilities will not do between two such as we. Are you quite positive? Come, let me look at you!"

"*Had* told you so? You only just asked and I only just answered!"

But his protests were nothing compared to Lady Madge's determination. "You have forgot! It was the first thing that came to mind on seeing you, to discover if you had come to any harm." She had assumed the role of ministering angel and so it should be. She took a dainty scrap of yellow silk from her reticule and began to dab at the worst of the grime on his face.

"I see no blood. Perhaps you are quite well after all. Are you sure? You have no idea how you frightened me, falling down that steep mountain-side like that! What an odd appearance you made, your clothes all over with dirt and even torn! And your face! You quite look like a laborer. You should not do such things to me. The shock, the surprise! I was near to fainting."

It took Kit some minutes to convince the lady that he was indeed in the peak of health and had suffered no harm from his scramble over the pike. The comment that it wasn't even a climb drew only a blank stare, and he gave up trying to explain to her that it had been merely a pike, not a summit or mountain range. That seemed beyond her comprehension. And she soon gave up trying to effect an improvement in his appearance. The square of silk was hopelessly inadequate.

Soon the whole episode of his descent down the fell was forgotten. Even his attire was scrupulously ignored by his companion, and she began to talk to him in an animated fashion on topics commonplace and dull.

"Isn't this the most exhilarating and picturesque view you have ever observed?" she said. "I was terribly clever to think of meeting you here."

Kit cast a doubtful eye in the direction of the peaks. They had completely disappeared into the clouds. Somehow it didn't seem like the sort of thing that would suit Lady Madge. "Just why did you come up to Cumberland?" he asked hastily.

"To be able to share such an experience with you, my beloved, is rapture. I couldn't stay away. Aren't you pleased that I was able to make my way north? Do tell me you are! I know what is in your heart, but to hear the words from your own sweet lips would be such bliss!"

"Lady Madge, just why did you come?" he asked again.

This time she took her cue. "Why, to be near you, darling! I couldn't bear to be so far from all I cared for! You are the most important person in my life, Kit, dearest, you know that. I had to come! If the Sopthwaites hadn't offered me a way, I would have found another! I would have walked those long miles, if necessary, just to see you! You must know that!"

Kit's face began to burn as he heard these endearments, spoken in a louder voice than usual, and he found himself looking over his shoulder, hoping that no one would come upon them.

"Madge, that's all well and good, but . . ."

"Tell me you love me, dearest Kit!" she teased.

He stumbled over the words. "Madge, I'm dashed fond of you, very fond. You're one of my dearest friends."

She bit her lip, then smiled gently, some of her poise returning. "Such a shy boy. One of your dearest friends! Am I? You are too embarrassed to speak the truth that is in your heart! Let us speak no more of whys and wherefores. Let us enjoy the grandeur of the scenery around us, share this soul-inspiring experience. We have been apart for so long!"

"It's dashed difficult for me to be here, Madge. I can't stay long, you know."

It was as if she hadn't heard him. "We shall reestablish our rapport, the unity of our spirits in these harmonious surroundings! That will be just the thing."

"Madge, the mist is rolling in, you ought to get back down to Grassmere, don't you think?"

"Darling, where is your mirror? We shall share the same view, the two of us side by side."

"Mirror?"

She shook her head. "You naughty boy, you forgot!"

"Mirror!"

"Kit, dear, I quite understand why you were unable to bring it with you. It would have broken in your fall! But never fear, you shall share mine with me! Isn't that better?"

He stared at her in disbelief as she drew her own mirror from the reticule dangling at her wrist and turned her back to the valley scene below. The small handbag was of blue silk, matching the silk of her dress and hat. Even her impractical shoes were the exact shade of blue. The scrap of yellow was the only source of contrast.

In a moment she was exclaiming with delight at the oval scene of the waterfall just across the way, and the way the water shone in her mirror glimmering dully.

"Do see, Kit. It is perfection! I can't wait to tell my friends in London about it! Perfection." She was in raptures, the scene was the epitome of all that was tasteful, the experience sublime. "Do come take a peek, dearest boy! Isn't it fortunate that I brought my oval mirror? The rectangular one would not have done half as well. There is a charm to the oval frame that is quite distinctive. I must just mention it to Mr. Sopthwaite."

"I'm pleased you are enjoying yourself so much," Kit said with a sudden, rueful calm.

"Do come and look!"

Pulling a sturdy linen handkerchief from his pocket, he wiped his face, then answered. "No, thank you. I prefer to see my views with my own eyes, not through a mirror."

"But this is the tasteful way to see the view! Everybody says so! Mr. Ackermann recommends it in his lovely volume, I'm sure someone has told me so."

"Undoubtedly he does, but I shall choose my own way, thank you just the same."

"Well, suit yourself," she said doubtfully. "But when you get back to London people will think your trip a poor affair indeed if you tell them you didn't use a mirror. Everyone is doing so."

"Yes, well, about London . . ."

"It has been a desert without you! I don't know how I've survived all alone."

"I'm sorry that you were lonely."

"I have tried to forget my desolation as best I could, after all, you have had the worst of it, stranded up here in these desolate mountains."

"Fells."

"Whatever they are!"

She had left him at a loss for words. How could he tell her of his resolve?

"About your news," he ventured.

"News?"

"Yes, your letter mentioned some important news. What is your surprise?"

"Oh, well, I wonder that I should tell you at all!"

"It was the reason for our meeting, I thought."

"The reason? Ridiculous! I couldn't live without seeing your dear face, that is why I sought this meeting. Letters are such dry things!" She dabbed at her eyes with her yellow handkerchief, then stopped when she realized how soiled it was. A frown puckered her mouth as she stared down at it.

"I cannot live without you," she muttered.

Kit picked up the oval mirror and handed it back to her, every gesture slow and gentle. "Do share your surprise with me! I would truly like to know what it is."

"It is hardly a surprise, I suppose, Kit. It is just that Rudolph, my husband Rudolph . . ."

"Yes."

"He has left me. He has returned to the Continent."

"I'm so sorry, Madge, but isn't that for the best? The two of you have never gotten along, never been close! It is years since you ceased to care for him. You told me so yourself!"

"But Kit, how can you suggest such a thing! For the best? He has humiliated me before the Ton! He ran off with some little dancer or actress or someone of that sort!"

He sighed and suppressed the impulse to remind the lady of her own friendship with a certain young man.

"That must have been a terrible blow."

"Terrible! Everyone is laughing at me!"

"Then it is well that you were able to visit the Lake District. Talk will have died down by the time you return to town."

"Yes, exactly. But Kit, it is worse than that!" She turned to him with red-rimmed eyes, their blue sheened with moisture. "Who is to take care of me, Kit? I am all alone now."

"To all intents and purposes you were all alone before, Madge."

She grabbed at his hand, pulling against his instinctive recoil. "But darling, this is our chance! We can now go off together. Before I was concerned about Rudolph, I couldn't bear to be so cruel to him. But now there is no such barrier to our happiness! We might even purchase a divorce for me and then we could be married."

He was surprisingly calm as he answered her. "Madge, just think of the scandal. You would be turned away from every respectable home in London! You can't be serious!"

"Scandal? What do I care of scandal?"

"Madge, you told me yourself that I must fulfill my responsibilities!"

"You have a responsibility to me, Kit! I love you!" The tone of her voice was imperceptibly failing to match the softness of her words and look. Recognizing the glint of steel he was altogether too familiar with in his own mother, Kit sighed with relief. Lady Madge, whatever her difficulties, was still Lady Madge, a woman he now saw with clear eyes.

"And I shall always save a very special place for

you in my heart, darling. But I must have a care for my position, for the people who depend on me."

"You didn't do so before! You have changed. I sensed that there was something different about you when I first saw you coming down that hill."

"And I have you to thank for showing me how foolish I was. You did me the greatest possible service when you made me face my responsibilities! I must begin to be the man, not the boy, and I owe this realization to you. I shall be eternally grateful."

"But . . ."

"Now we must part for ever, Madge. I shall be spending more of my time here in Cumberland, now that I'm approaching my majority."

"In Cumberland?"

"Yes. London will rarely see me," he explained with sardonic pleasure. He could see her squirming at the thought.

"This is your mother speaking, surely! You can't be saying such things. I know you too well!"

"Madge, it is *you* speaking! Saying those dear, wise things to me back in London. My life lies here and I shall forever honor you for being brave enough to convince me of that."

It was now Lady Madge's turn to see determination in the other's tone and face. It was a show of strength wholly new and unusual in him, for she had always had everything her way in the past. It caused her to pause and consider what she had best do.

After a long, tense moment, she smiled and shed another tear. "How brave you are, Kit darling. Brave and wise. I shall always love you for this, always cherish you."

"You should congratulate yourself, Madge. I owe it all to you," he murmured with some truth.

"But there are so many practical details that I must now cope with, now that Rudolph has gone! I am overwhelmed by them!"

Kit hesitated a moment, then stiffened. "Perhaps your new friend Mr. Sopthwaite could assist you with them? I shall be buried here in the north, it would be difficult for me to be of much assistance to you in London. But if he resides there for much of the year, surely you could turn to him? And he sounds the sort who would have a much better head for business than I."

He watched her while she considered all this, then added something to clinch the argument. "Someone as precious and fragile as you, should be relying on older and wiser heads than mine. I'm a mere stripling, you know. You need a stronger arm to lean on, stronger than I can provide."

"Nonsense! Your arm is strong, I'm sure! It is quite heroic in strength." She said this in an absentminded way. As she grew accustomed to this change in her life, coming so fast on her husband's departure, but with the prospect of a new protector, a wealthy one, seeming better and better, the old Lady Madge began to assert herself. "But if you won't be about London as much as before, I very much fear that I shall have to turn to Mr. Sopthwaite. If you are sure?"

"I shall be there very little, I assure you."

"And it is true that you have only just begun to

assume so many new responsibilities, such that will quite take all your time and attention."

"I shall be overwhelmed!"

"Then I shall just ask dearest Mr. Sopthwaite for a word or two of advice on occasion."

"An excellent notion!"

"Not that he will ever mean as much to me as you."

"You honor me!"

"And dearest Kit."

"Yes, Madge?"

"I shall always cherish your memory, deep in my heart."

"And I yours."

Sixteen

As Kit retraced his route over the pike, he turned over in his mind his handling of so delicate a situation. On the whole, he was pleased with himself. He had seen the light just in time. It had been foolishly naive of him to place such great faith in the depths of Madge's devotion. Only a chuckle brain would have accepted her protestations of love for true, deep emotion. He doubted that she would ever be capable, had ever been capable, of anything more than empty protestations.

He thought of her efforts to forget his absence from London, a rueful chuckle rising in him. He doubted that she had missed him at all in town. She had come north because it was the fashionable thing to do, or because the trip (if his guess was correct) had been paid for by another, or because she was anxious to be certain of her next protector now that her erstwhile husband was gone. Or perhaps because of all these reasons.

Yes, he'd done quite well. Scrambling over the scree, he congratulated himself on his inspiration. He had said what was needed, that was the important thing. After all, *he* had cared, even if she had not. And yes, Mr. Sopthwaite was the very thing for Madge. He would do well by her, Kit was sure. He only hoped that Mrs. Sopthwaite didn't mind too much.

It was surprising that such a small thing as a mirror could be so handy. Handier than Madge ever imagined, with all her prattlings of views and inspiration and grandeur. It had framed a very thought-provoking picture for Kit to see. There had been something in the way it reflected her eyes that had told him the truth. For all her exclaiming over the beauties of the mountainside and valley and mere, she had not been truly looking at them, nor at him. She had been looking at herself. He guessed that she was communing with herself, with some part of her soul that only she could see. How could such a woman truly love, truly give her heart?

He was beginning to slide down the other side of the pike when he was disconcerted to hear voices below him. A couple, a man and a woman, were talking down there. Or rather arguing. Yes, the man's voice boomed up carrying a note of irritation, even a hint of threat in its timber. And the woman's? The woman's voice was little more than that of a girl, high and sweet. The tones sounded terribly familiar. He found himself straining to eavesdrop on just what was being said. That voice . . .

The voice was Kitty's! And she was crying out for help!

Any sense of climbing skill deserted him and he tumbled across the sharp stones without heeding the cuts and scratches they inflicted. Desperate, he took the last few hundred feet headlong, ending up on the spot where he had left Kitty less than an hour before.

But Kitty wasn't there.

"Kitty, where are you? What's happening? For God's sake, answer me!" he bellowed.

A muffled oath could be heard around the curve in the path, a curve seemingly blocked by rockslide.

"Kitty, are you over there?"

He could hear another oath, then a scream was cut off abruptly. What was happening to Kitty? How had she gotten on the other side of a solid wall of rock and dirt? Furious, sure that she had been kidnapped, carried off by force, Kit attacked the pile of rubble and stones with demonic energy. He must get to her!

The loose dirt slipped out from under his feet, denying him a path over the slide, but he ignored this constantly unwilling retreat. Only his irrational fear for the girl got him over the rockslide, for nature and gravity were working against him. With a strength he had never before found in himself, he propelled himself over the top to the other side of the path inspired by sheer anger.

The scene there was even worse than he had expected to meet. Kitty was on the ground, crying, a man in some sort of uniform standing over her, licking his hand.

"Damned wench! That time you drew blood, good and proper. A simple 'no' would have been sufficient!" he grumbled.

"Who are you? What have you done to her! Stand about and face me, you cur, you have met with justice!" Without stopping to compare his opponent's taller frame and heavier arms and shoulders with his own slender physique, Kit charged to a position before him. With one anxious glance down at the girl, he stepped between her and her tormenter.

"So this is the lad you've been saving yourself for, eh? Sweet Jesus, the place seems to be crawling with bumpkins. What are you, anyway, a shepherd? A goatherd? You look like worse."

Kit ignored this slur and raised his clenched fist as he had been taught to do in Gentleman Jackson's Salon. "Kitty, are you hurt? Has he done you some harm? What happened?" He contrived to glance down at her and keep an eye on the stranger by bobbing his eyes back and forth.

"Nothing happened," the officer answered in a sullen voice. "And don't make such a fool of yourself as to raise your hand to me. I don't fight with farmhands or miners. The silly wench lost her head, that was all. I did nothing."

Kit's fists remained raised.

"Kitty?"

"I am all right, Kit. He has only frightened me badly, and I fear I have gathered a bruise or two, but mostly from falling down the slide."

"He flung you to the ground like a rag doll,

damn him! I shall teach him a lesson he'll never forget."

"Please don't fight him, Kit! It would only cause a scandal. Please!"

"I can ignore the insults he has aimed against me, but I cannot ignore his torment of you. Sir, are you willing to fight?"

"With an oaf? And a stripling at that?" The man threw back his head and laughed.

"I will not permit you to leave here without satisfaction. You shall fight whether you choose or no."

"Kit, no! Someone might get hurt!"

But by now the two men were ignoring the girl, letting her scramble to her feet without assistance.

"Stand off!"

Kit sneered back in his face, then began circling his opponent. "Kitty, keep back."

She looked at the anger on the men's faces, and with a sigh, did as she was told.

"And no, sir, we shall settle the question of this dishonorable conduct of yours here and now," Kit said with all the arrogance of generations of de Flemings behind him.

"Damn you, you young pup, I'll not fight you," the other man snarled. "But I shall take great pleasure in teaching you a lesson!"

A very large fist, propelled by a massive shoulder and arm, flashed out across the space between the opponents. It connected with the stubborn jaw of Kitty's protector, lifting him off his feet in such a way that he fell to the ground.

"Kit! He has hurt you!" She knelt beside her fallen friend, then turned a withering, slightly teary glare at the officer. "You are a brute, and not a gentleman at all."

He was flexing his right hand with some care, his brow still lowering. "Young fool!" he muttered. "Your wench's bites and kicks had already made the point and driven me off. Why did you have to go and ask for worse from me? If anyone should receive a crown of laurels for their fighting today, it's this silly chit." And with that he stalked back down the path to Grassmere.

It took Kitty some time to make Kit comfortable. By ripping her petticoat she was able to provide bandages to bind his swelling face and clean his person. Between the blood of his confrontation and his too-hasty journey over the pike, he was a sorry sight. Bemused, Kit watched this efficient nursing, far more effective than the ministrations provided by a yellow silk handkerchief.

"You are so very brave, to stand up for me like that! So very brave to defend me!" Kitty whispered over and over as she worked. It was the best balm she could have provided.

"The damned scoundrel. I shall have him removed from his regiment. Treating a lady in such a manner!"

"He was rather dreadful, but he didn't really hurt me, just frightened me terribly!"

"That is more than enough reason for the worst possible punishments! Are you sure you are quite all right?"

"Yes, of course, it is you who have been hurt. How gallant of you to face him like that! He a larger man and a professional soldier, accustomed to all sorts of rough sports and fighting, and you exhausted by your long climb. Kit, you were magnificent! Truly magnificent!"

Kit tried to give her a deprecating grin, then groaned as his tortured face protested. "Hardly that. I seem to have ended on the ground. Not magnificent at all."

"No, you did something more important than that! You defended me. That is very precious to me. I used to think that officers must be gentlemen and paragons of chivalry! Like knights riding into tournaments for their ladies' favors. But this shows me how wrong I was."

"I still feel a dashed fool!"

"No, don't! You have shown me that there is more to being a gentleman than simple brute prowess and military rank. You have shown me the true qualities that make a man chivalrous and a gentleman. You are quite a hero!"

For a moment he doubted her sincerity. How could one be heroic while lying flat on one's back? With the lady he was defending ministering to him because he was too helpless to help himself? And after her attacker had given her the honors for the day's fighting? It was too humiliating. But her voice was sincere, her touch gentle. He began to believe that she might mean what she said.

"I couldn't bear the thought of him hurting you. Or even treating you in so disrespectful a manner," he murmured to her. "I only wish I had better represented you. I wanted to win the fight for your sake!"

"Oh, Kit, you may not have won this fight, but you win all the others! The important ones that call for a different sort of courage and strength than that lout demonstrated. You have the courage that counts, the courage that makes you defend the right without thinking of yourself."

Now he was not only convinced that she wasn't teasing him in an effort to soothe his damaged pride, he was embarrassed by the effusion of her admiration.

"Dash it all, Kitty, it was nothing. Nothing! Any chap would do the same!"

"Say what you will, I know different."

Feeling more alert, and anxious to turn the talk away from himself, Kit sat up and tried to take stock of their surroundings. "Kitty, how did you come to get over here?"

"I climbed over the slide. It was easy that first time. But then I couldn't get back."

"But why?"

"I wanted to see if I could find a fuller view of the waterfall!"

"The waterfall?" He turned toward the valley, his eyes searching for the force of water. The view was shrouded in mist. "Dash it all, Kitty! The mist is thickening. And fast! We shall have to get back to the others."

"Yes, of course. I shall gave you my arm to lean on."

She helped him to his feet and they turned to the path. It was blocked by an even greater pile of loose rubble. Kit's attack on the slide had worsened it. They were silent as they stared at their obstacle.

"We shall have to go back the other way. Take the trod into Grassmere and find our way home from there."

"It is so infuriating! Our friends and family but a few yards away, less than a mile, and inaccessible! They might as well be in another world!" the girl wailed.

"It can't be helped."

"Do you feel well enough to walk so far? I could go ahead for help!"

Vivid memories of what had already come of leaving Kitty unprotected flashed through Kit's mind and he set his jaw in a tender but determined line. "No, we shall stay together. I shan't let you out of my sight, not a second time. Not ever again!"

She had turned to face the direction they must take, and, dismayed by what she saw, missed that there was something more than determination in his voice. "We shall not be able to see but a few feet ahead of us, Kit. We might lose our way."

"Nonsense!" he said bracingly. "We shall simply follow the trod. That is easy enough."

"I hope so," she answered in a quiet voice as she took his arm firmly in hers. "We can only do our best."

Seventeen

As the picnic party saw the hour of noon approach and pass, it was decided by Mrs. Brampton to send a servant along the path to fetch back Kit and Kitty from their ramble.

"Isn't it charming that they get along so well?" Mrs. de Fleming cooed from her comfortable seat in the shade. "They are made for one another, I knew it the moment I saw them standing side by side. Although it is frightfully naughty of them to stay away so long."

Mrs. Brampton, irritated that she was facing a considerable delay in her planned luncheon hour, and reserving the right of criticism to herself, ignored the last of this speech. "Nonsense. You had them matched before you ever saw Kitty, much less put the two of them side by side. Kitty's fortune was enough for you."

"Well, really now, you make me sound a perfect mercenary! As if I would never consider Kit's happiness in advising him in such an important decision."

"I wonder that the footman is so long coming back," Mrs. Leyburne fretted. Unlike the other two ladies, she was worried about neither ideal matches nor her lunch. "It is ages since he set out!"

"Dallying along the way, I'll warrant," Mrs. Brampton rumbled.

"Hardly that. He is a most reliable man. I do so hope nothing has happened to the young people."

"Happened? Nonsense, what could befall them?" Mrs. de Fleming asked in a manner to imply a negative answer as the obvious right one.

"Oh, an accident, perhaps."

"I do hope that that Kit of yours is entirely reliable. He seemed to behave very oddly earlier in the day. Most odd, his wandering off like that, pretending not to hear you when you called him back."

"Well, really, I do hope that I, as Kit's mother, can understand him better than a mere stranger. La! He is young and in love . . ."

"Posh!"

"And has his head in the clouds in consequence. There is no possibility that he would ignore his mother, I can assure you. Not with deliberate intent."

"Be that as it may, is he reliable?"

There was a chilling silence. "Reliable?"

"He has taken Kitty off on some hare-brained adventure, I'll warrant."

"Surely not, Mrs. Brampton," Mrs. Leyburne interposed hastily. "They have jaunted off before and come to no harm."

"Well then, why did you raise the alarm?"

"Yes, Mrs. Leyburne, it was you who first voiced fears for their safety," Mrs. de Fleming agreed with a sudden shift of allegiance.

"In the past they have always returned in good time. I'm sure that no fault can be laid at your son's door, Mrs. de Fleming. That was all I intended to say."

"Such a start over nothing!" the fond mother snapped back.

"It is just that the mist is gathering in the valley bottom. I thought perhaps it would be thick in other places, too. Perhaps they have lost their way in the mist."

There was a long, considering silence, then Mrs. Brampton struck. "You are being very brave to say such things, to hide your real fear. But I know what is in the back of your mind. What would be in the back of any mother's mind when her daughter, a girl of tender years, has been sent off on a stroll with an adventurer and not returned in good time! You fear that Kitty has met with worse than misadventure!"

"Adventurer? What are you saying about my precious son?" Mrs. de Fleming shrilled. For the first time since their arrival at the clearing she was on her feet, facing Mrs. Brampton. "My Kit is a good boy. A gentleman, the heir to a title! How dare you?"

"The heir to a penniless title," Mrs. Brampton rumbled back, a malicious smile on her face.

"But a gentleman of lineage, none the less. More than can be said of the Bramptons of the world. Corruption of Broughton! Pah! That is absurd!"

"Ladies, ladies, please, people can hear you!" Mrs. Leyburne pleaded. "And look! The mist is rolling over the valley now. Positively rolling in and filling it up. My darling must be lost out there some place. Lost!"

It is doubtful that her sensible intervention, even coupled as it was with heartfelt anguish, could have separated the two angry women. That the fog was thickening, that a serious accident might have occurred to the young people, these were nothing compared to the insults that had been exchanged.

The battle was prevented by the reappearance of the young footman who had been sent out on the search.

"Thank God, John, you have come back! What has happened? Has one of them been injured?" Mrs. Leyburne demanded.

"Injured? Well, ma'am, it's not me who can say for sure."

"Where are they? Where is dearest Kitty?" Mrs. Brampton asked the man.

"Kitty? What of my Kit?"

This apparition of motherly fury took away what few words John possessed. It was only Mrs. Leyburne's intervention that ignited the spark of sense in his brain, for of all the ladies there, she was the most familiar, the one who owned his allegiance, and the only one making any sense.

"What do you mean, John? What did you find?"

"I found naught, mum."

"Naught?" screeched Mrs. de Fleming.

"Naught. Nothing. He has said that he didn't find them, you silly chit." This from Mrs. Brampton.

"How dare you?"

"John, if there was no sign of them, what could have happened?" Mrs. Leyburne asked, near tears.

"I don't know. I follows the trod to the very end of its way, as I was told to do. There were no sign of the young couple along it, no other trod for they to follows. They do disappear into the mist, they do. Mum." The last was added as an afterthought, for his mother had drilled him in strict courtesy, and now that he had said his piece, his mind was returning to practical concerns, such as steady employment. This disaster boded ill for all.

Mrs. Brampton was listening to him again, her back turned to Mrs. de Fleming.

"That is impossible! Disappeared?"

"Impossible? Not at all. That wretched girl has led my poor boy over some precipice, I'll wager!"

"She has led him? Surely you have confused the issue. He has led her!"

"John, was there no where they could have gone?"

"No, mum. The path, it did end in a slide. I tried to get across, but can't be done. None could have gone thataway."

Mrs. Leyburne vainly searched her mind for an explanation to this mystery, ignoring the bickering that still raged behind her. If the path lacked any sidetracks, if it ended in a blockage that withstood the assault of a sturdy countryman such as John, where could the children be? Oh, please, dear Lord, where could they be? she prayed fervently.

Then Mrs. Brampton's voice overrode her thoughts and she was forced to listen.

"If anyone has been led over the edge of a cliff, it was poor, dear Kitty. And the man who led her was Kit!"

"There be naught more we can do, mum, not in this thick weather." John's worried voice finally penetrated Mrs. Leyburne's paralyzing fears. "You ladies best be back to the Hall afore it worsen and trap us all up here."

With a start, Mrs. Leyburne realized that some minutes had passed since Mrs. Brampton's announcement and that the clearing was beginning to fill with mist. "What? Return? Without them?"

"The master can set out search parties from there. He can call on plenty to help. I'll stay hereabouts and see if I can find more, mum. They probably just took a tumble and had a bit of a slide, like."

"Did you shout for them?"

The man squirmed with embarrassment. "Well, mum, yas, I did do that."

Shutting her mind as to why he received no answer, she nodded her head vaguely. "We shall return to the Hall. Have the other servants pack up the baskets, John. There is no point in all of us being lost in this fog. And you are right. My husband is the best person to deal with this." With a new air of resolve, she turned to her companions. "Mrs. de Fleming. Mrs. Brampton.

You must stop this foolish argument and return with me to the Hall. The sooner we arrive there, the sooner the search can begin. There is nothing else to be done!"

Eighteen

They hadn't known they were lost until they found themselves slipping down the north face of a fell.

"Mungo has told me many times to turn south when I'm on an unfamiliar fell," Kitty remarked with a giggle when they had fetched up on a narrow ledge and were peering into the mist below.

Exhausted as he was, Kit realized that the laughter was rooted in panic that approached hysteria, and he gave her a reassuring pat. "Who's to say we aren't doing just that? In this mist no one can tell north from south, east from west, without a compass!"

"Oh, no, we've gone north."

"Oh, come Kitty, how can you tell?"

"The north side of fells are always, or almost always, rocky, with steep faces."

"Good grief."

"No, it's true."

"And the southern faces?"

"They are usually smoother, gentler, with less of a sharp decline."

Kit, relieved that the delivery of this prosaic information seemed to have taken the edge from her voice, looked around them with a gloomy shake of his head. "Then we are most definitely on the northern face! I have never seen a steeper climb."

Kitty nodded her agreement. "It seems so."

He twisted about to peer down into the mist as far as he could, then asked, "What of that stream bed we passed a few feet back? Perhaps we could follow it down? It seems to be the only route left to us. I think we could find it if we retreated along this path."

"No, never follow a beck down, only up."

"More of Mungo's wisdom?"

"Of course. Some of the streams have steep waterfalls. If you don't know your way along them, and can't see too clearly to boot, you're liable to step over one without realizing what's happened."

"When you hit the bottom you'd know." Now the despair was in Kit's voice.

"Why don't we just huddle here until the mist rises?" Kitty suggested after a moment. "It ought to do so soon. I feel the wind coming up."

"No, I can't let you stay out here in this miserable fog, sitting on a rocky ledge overlooking what is undoubtedly a hundred-foot drop. Besides, we might be stuck here all night if we don't do something about it." He began to struggle to his feet, only to be pulled back by his companion.

"Kit, you must rest. You have done too much already."

"Nonsense, I . . ."

She tugged ruthlessly at his arm. "Don't be silly. It will do me no good if you slip and hurt yourself even more seriously, or if you simply collapse from exhaustion."

He opened his mouth to argue further, then shut it with a grimace of pain.

"And your jaw is terribly swollen, perhaps even cracked or broken, and it must be paining you terribly. Do let's just sit and rest for the moment. We can afford to wait a few hours, it won't be much past two o'clock by now. There are many more hours of sunlight."

She was right, the pain in his jaw was more than he could stand, and he sank back against the mossy rock at his back. Seeing she had gained an advantage, she pressed on.

"See, the wind is freshening. It will blow away this mist in no time. There is no point in wandering about if you don't know where to go, is there?"

"No, you're right. We'll just go in circles, as we have been for the past two hours. I'm a fine guide, aren't I?"

"Don't be silly!" Shyly, she slipped her hand into his and cuddled against his shoulder. "Everything will be just fine. What else can go wrong?"

Nineteen

The sound of bells rolled eerily through the thinning mist. Kitty awoke with a start. It seemed as if the chimes came from another world. It couldn't be that help was at hand!

"Is anybody there?" she shouted.

"What? What are you saying? Where are we?" Kit stirred groggily from his exhausted slumber and sought to gain his feet. Kitty pushed him back down onto the moss.

"There is someone nearby! They will help us or go and get help, I am sure."

"Let me take care of this."

"No, no, you are too exhausted. Sit back." Again she shoved him down.

"Hello! Help! Is there anyone about? Please answer, we need your help."

A dim rumble could be heard from immediately beneath them.

"What? What did you say?" the girl called out. "We are perched up on this ledge. Can you help us down?"

The words, spoken in the rich, local accents, were suddenly clear. "Ledge? Ter ain't no ledge up there. Step down yerselves!" The advice was followed by an explosion of laughter.

"What?" The couple peered into the lessening mists, trying to make out just what it was they had heard. Surely the voice couldn't have said what it did?

It had. As the mist fast disappeared, they saw that they were but a few feet from the valley floor. With the aid of a sturdy bush that jutted out near them, they would have no trouble lowering themselves down to safety.

Before they could effect their own rescue, an evil, leering grin floated into view. A man whose appearance epitomized all that they had imagined a vicious, lawless smuggler would be was standing a few paces down a trod, his hand holding the reins of a pack pony.

"Hee, hee! Ye sat on that there ledge in sheer fright, did ye? Hee, hee!"

As he slapped his side and doubled over with more laughter, the sinister impression he had made on them disappeared with the last of the mist. Instead, there stood below them a respectable pony driver, dressed roughly, it was true, but leading a small beast properly belled and burdenless to boot. Just because he was laughing at them was no reason to assume he was a smuggler or any other sort of outlaw—far from it.

"Step ye down, step ye down," he insisted, sounding for all the world like a host welcoming guests into his parlor. With two strong arms he set Kitty on her feet in the thick grass of the trod. "There ye be, missy, there ye be. Safe and sound. Or my name ain't Jocky Treslow."

"See, Kit, I told you everything would work out!" Kitty announced triumphantly as she turned to her friend. Then a look of fright covered her face, for Kit was falling off the ledge, apparently in a dead faint.

The lush grass and the pony man's arms prevented any serious injury befalling the youth, but not even water from the man's canteen could revive him.

"Oh, please, put him on your pony and help me take him to my parents' house! My father will pay you well for it."

Jocky Treslow stared contemptuously at her torn dress and tear-stained face, then cocked his ear to catch the sounds of her cultured voice the better.

"Pay me, will he?" He looked her over yet again, then shook his head.

"Please, he is Mr. Leyburne of the Hall. He will reward you handsomely for rescuing us."

"That may well be, missy, but what of my own master? What of he?"

"Your master? Surely he couldn't object to your helping us!"

"Oh, he cud, missy, he cud. You don' know the Ole Master. He be like ole Baldy. He expects what be due him, he does. There ain't no way of shirkin' him."

"But you can't just leave us here!"

"Nay, that be true. Not fitty that weren't. Not decent." He appeared to consider the problem for a moment, then stooped down and hauled Kit up in his arms.

"Put the lad's leg over the pony's back, missy. Then you do walk on the one side and me the other. We'll keep him on her thataway."

"Then you *are* taking us home!" Kitty exclaimed gratefully as she assisted him with his plan. In a moment Kit was leaning against the pony's neck and the driver had taken up the lead reins once again.

"Oh, aye, I be takin' you home. It be the only thin' to do, if only the master won't be angered."

"It is so kind of you!"

They were passing through the spray of the waterfall when Kitty looked up and recognized the peak overhead. The mist parted to reveal a rugged profile of unique juts and cuts.

They were going in the wrong direction.

"This isn't the way to the Hall! Where are you taking us?"

"Course not! It be the way home!"

"But we must get Kit to help. Someone must go for a doctor. . . ."

"Oh, aye, the master will see to that."

"But Mr. de Fleming's mother is at the Hall. She will want to care for him herself. He needs the most immediate and careful attention."

The worthy stopped to glare at her over the pony's nose. "A body kin see that! Betimes, what happened to the lad? All punished in the face? And the two of you? How you come to be lost and lookin' dirty for all your fine way of talkin'?"

"That isn't important. My father will be very angry that you haven't carried us straight back to the Hall. And he is a magistrate, too! He will have you brought into his court for not getting Kit to treatment quickly!"

"I be getting the lad to whatever it is that you called it, missy. He'll git patched up. And quick, too. Home be nearer than the Hall. Anybody kin see that."

"But a doctor, nursing? Can I rely . . ." She got no further.

"I tell ye, the Ole Master, he see to that. At least I suppose he will."

"You can only suppose? Where are you taking us? This can't be happening to us! Who is your master?"

But the pony driver had turned surly. Perhaps her threats of magisterial fury had turned him unfriendly, perhaps he doubted her ability to see him well rewarded if he complied with her demands, for in truth she and Kit were a sorry-looking pair. Or memories of his master's past wrath could have left him frightened. But for the rest of their uneven journey, he refused to gainsay her so much as another word.

Kitty was left to pray that the Ole Master, whoever he might be, would be kindlier than his servant.

Twenty

There were still wisps of fog shrouding the valley they at last turned into. As she stared down at the jumble of buildings below her, Kitty's heart was in her mouth, for in the late afternoon, the rays of the sun were cut off by the lips of an overhanging peak and the scene was shrouded in shifting darkness.

There rose from the valley floor a building that was part pele, part badstofa, and part Elizabethan manorhouse. The tower, square and grim, stood guarding the entrance to the valley, still prepared as it had been for centuries to blunt the attack of invaders. Once it had sheltered fleeing farm folk, their supplies and goods stored in the vaulted ground floor, the lookout and defense organized in the narrow-windowed room above this, and a living room of sorts for all the villagers in the floor yet higher. Centuries before, warning of danger had been given by the lights of beacon fires that flashed notice of invaders across the countryside. With a shiver Kitty took in the rough-pocked surface of the walls of the tower, blank except for the rare slits that served as windows and apertures for the archers aiming at the enemy below. The sunlight burning on the top of the tower failed to soften the dismal melancholy, for it gave the structure the aspect of a flaming brand.

Behind the tower, incorporating its grim strength into a more gracious mode, rambled an Elizabethan manor of the sort Kitty was familiar with. The windows were many and diamond-paned, the lines of the door and roof graceful and generous, and there was even a hint of ancient topiary in what was left of the grounds before it, but the omnious tower destroyed what charm it might have possessed.

The more she observed, the more Kitty felt that she had stumbled into a giants' nursery and encountered their efforts with building blocks. Tossed to one side there were the remains of a wattle-and-daub farmhouse running into the hillside, obviously of earlier date than the main house. Judging from the smoke pouring from its round cumbrian chimneys it was still in use, perhaps the badstofa still serving its ancient function as a dormitory for the domestic servants.

A low moan from Kit demanded all her attention and she stretched to slip her arm around his waist. She found herself answering not his incoherent questions but the tone of fear and confusion in his voice.

"It's all right, Kit, dear, everything is all right. We're coming to some sort of farmhouse right now."

"Kitty? You're all right? I had a terrible dream that I had fought someone . . ." His voice failed as a lurch from the pony deprived him of breath.

"Yes, everything is all right now. It wasn't a dream, you did fight someone. But we're on our way to help now. We're almost there. See the valley?"

It was at this moment that the setting sun chose to effect a lighting display that highlighted the patchwork qualities of the house. The shafts of light broke over the edge of the pike, jabbing between breaks in its rocky surface, casting a weird, mismatched appearance over the far side of the valley where the buildings stood. Odd shadows were dominated by brilliant splashes of sunlight which blinded the eyes of the little party traveling in that direction. With a moan, Kit turned his head away.

"Where are we, Kitty? That cannot be Leyburne Hall, except in some nightmare. It's all wrong, all wrong."

"This is a nearer dwelling. The man who is helping us thought it would enable you to reach help faster if we came straight here."

"But Kitty, the sun is setting! You, I mean, *we* can't spend the night together in some strange, deserted tower!"

"Tain't deserted!" the pony driver muttered. "There be a warm fire and a platter full of food there, young master. Just you see."

"Yes, Kit, there is smoke coming from the chimneys. You mustn't worry yourself."

"Mustn't worry myself? Kitty, you can't spend the night here, you mustn't. It's impossible! What will your mother say?"

"My mama will be pleased that we have spent the night safely, in shelter with kind, respectable neighbors."

"Kind? Respectable? How can you be sure?"

"Kit, please, we must stay here. There is no place else for us to go!" she pleaded.

"But your parents! My mother! Mrs. Brampton!" His voice trailed off into a groan that had only partly to do with the pain in his head and jaw.

Their arrival had been noted and the great door of the hall, the smaller recessed door of the farmhouse wing, all the sheds and barns, had been flung open and a crowd of people descended on them. The pony driver dropped the reins of his small animal and ambled on ahead, allowing the beast and its burden to follow at a slower pace while Jock enjoyed the role of harbinger of news and gossip.

Kit was still mumbling and groaning and Kitty threw a despairing glance toward the approaching group. "Please, Kit, they will hear! We mustn't offend them," she whispered, casting him a beseeching look. She needn't have worried, for he had begun to slump into her arms once again and she realized that they were not to reach the front door of the manorhouse without help.

As she turned to the folk in the yard, wondering if they had noticed her plight and not sure if she should cry out for help, a tall figure emerged from the door of the manor. A shock of white hair fell over deep-set eyes and a beaky nose, and one autocratic finger directed the people's attention away from Jock and up the path. In a moment she was surrounded by help, the men seizing the injured Kit and bundling him onto a plank of wood, the women clustering around the girl. For better or worse, Kit and Kitty had found shelter for the night.

Twenty-one

Not even the bright sunlight streaming through the mullioned windows was sufficient to dispel the terror of the nightmare that had held Kit in its grip.

It had started with an alfresco party on the banks of the Thames, a pleasant enough enterprise, if a trifle dull. But the only two guests present were he and a lady in blue. He tried repeatedly to see the lady's face, and she kept turning her back on him with a laugh to praise the fine view she saw through her mirror. She held it so as to see over her shoulder the scene behind her, and it was in its reflection that he recognized the face of Lady Madge. He called her name, trying to walk around her to look directly at her, but she evaded him, spinning in an ever-faster circle. Then he had grabbed her arm to try to stop her, to make her stand still and listen to him. Just as he had thought to have achieved this, he looked up and realized that they were no longer in the gentle south of England. Far from it. They were perched precariously on the edge of a precipice overlooking a storm-tossed mere, the waves below eating away at the foot of the cliff until it began to crumble, and it was no longer Lady Madge standing there beside him, but a giant cavalry officer, his uniformed arm raised in a threat.

The earth spun, faster than the lady in blue had done before, and Kit was on the ground, trying to stop the mad whirling of his head, no, he was on his feet, running over a hill that kept disappearing beneath him. He knew that he must surmount the hill, for the lady in blue was now on its far side, and crying out for help.

As suddenly as he had found himself transported to the Lake Counties, he discovered that the hill was behind him. The lady was nowhere to be seen, the only evidence of life in the area being a pony, and for some reason he knew that if he could but mount it it would take him to the lady.

Kit had ridden horses all his life, the small pony should have been no challenge to him, but try as he might, he could not maintain his seat on the animal's back. As soon as he had a leg flung over it, he felt his balance fail and he slid toward the ground. It was the hill all over again, the earth coming up to greet him, the pony disappearing out from under him. And he must reach the lady, and explain something that was terribly important, so important that he couldn't bear to think of what words he would use when he saw her, couldn't even bear to frame the thought in his mind.

The pony had somehow carried him down a rough trod and was entering an unknown valley. Kit had had to cling to its mane with all the strength he possessed, for he slipped and nearly fell with each lurching step the animal took. Surely he would have fallen if the lady had not been there by his side all the while, steadying him and talking to him. It was odd that he hadn't noticed her there, for now he knew that she had never left him.

He tried to tell her his message, he knew it was vital that she hear it. At the sound of his first words she turned to look up and he was startled to see that she wasn't Lady Madge at all, she was Kitty, and suddenly it was the easiest thing in the world to talk to her, to explain how he felt. The words came effortlessly and he was just beginning to impart his secret, when an old man with strangely familiar eyes and a beak of a nose loomed in the path before them, pointing his finger at the young couple. Kit struggled to reach Kitty, struggled to keep the dark away, but failed. Darkness fell.

It hadn't really been darkness at all. Kit had merely begun to wake up, or so he had told himself when his eyes finally became unstuck with sleep. There he was in a comfortable bed with clean sheets in a neat, well-cared-for room in what was obviously a household of some pretention. And he was still gripped with fear.

It is only the nightmare, he reassured himself, sinking back into the comfort of the feather pillows. I had the most dashed awful nightmare, and now I'm awake and everything is fine.

But was it? He glanced around the room and saw that although well-appointed, it was unfamiliar to him. The view from the window showed him a fell and hillside that were also new. If everything was fine, where in the world was he?

Perhaps the dream had been more real than he wanted to believe. He cast into his memory, ruthlessly tearing at the dream and the remnants of yesterday's activities such as he could still recall.

The lady in blue had been real enough. He had seen Lady Madge, joining her at a viewpoint overlooking Grassmere at the appointed time. They had talked and he had wanted to say something important to her, something difficult, then he had found it wasn't necessary. The lady was well able to divine the truth from his flattering evasions and had adjusted herself accordingly. She would have no trouble taking care of herself.

What then of a giant officer with clenched fist? And hills that slipped away from beneath his feet as no earth was meant to do? Had the giant struck him? If his jaw offered true evidence, he had. But why? Why had it been so important to climb that hill? Who had been screaming for help on the other side?

No, no, he was confusing dream with reality. He had confused the sequence of events. He had hurried down the rocky side of the fell, anxious to reach Kitty, when he had heard her screaming for help. Yes, it had been she he was worried about, not Lady Madge. She was the one who was important. But on arriving where he had left her, he had been faced with a waking nightmare. The glade was empty. And Kitty's voice was on the other side of a rockslide that was determined to stop him. It had only been after he had hurled himself over it that he had found Kitty, and the officer, and then had indeed been stretched out on the ground by the other man's blow.

But the pony? The jingle of bells in the yard below his window gave him a clue. He must have heard that and incorporated it into the dream. He had no recollection of a ride on a pony.

Then he knew that he had in fact been on one the day before. Somehow he had found himself on a pony, walking into a tunnel that was gray and seemingly endless until it disappeared and they were entering a valley that held an eerie, haunted castle. Kitty had been at his side, and he had wanted to say something important to her, something he had been feeling for a long time, but there was danger for her and the old man had stopped him and he had been brought into this house.

There was enough left in his mind of the day's events for Kit to feel an overwhelming sense of guilt and dismay. His foolish rendezvous with Lady Madge had put Kitty into danger, terrible danger. It was all his fault that she had been left on the hillside alone, an easy prey for any passing ruffian. She should have had his presence to protect her, instead he was skulking with a married lady of questionable reputation, meeting her in a secret rendezvous. His conduct had been reprehensible, disgusting. Every sense of delicacy was revolted. What would everyone think of him? Mrs.

Leyburne? His mother? It had been shocking conduct for a gentleman.

His mind stopped as he tried to imagine his mother's reaction. For some reason he feared an explosion of her anger out of all proportion to the situation. If anyone should be angry with him, it was Mr. and Mrs. Leyburne, Kitty's parents. They were the aggrieved party, not Mrs. de Fleming. Deep in his heart he suspected that his mother would not care so much for the dishonor of his actions, but for their practical effect on the proposed betrothal.

There was left just one part of his dream unexplained. Had there truly been an old man coming between him and Kitty? He feared that his mind must be teasing him again. Or perhaps he suffered from amnesia. No, there was a clear image of an elderly man, tall and thin and a trifle stooped in the shoulders, taking command of the scene on the edge of the yard. Kit recalled the fellow's attire and guessed him to be the master of the place, and there had been much sense and goodwill in the man's attentions. He had seen the wounded youth into the house and beside a warming fire in a thrice. But there was still the feeling of forboding that clung to this memory, the feeling that there was some long-familiar danger lurking here.

His reverie was disturbed by the sound of the door opening. A neat maidservant peeked around the oaken planks, saw that he was awake, and entered with a brisk curtsey. In her hands she carried a ladened tray.

"Ole Master, he said you should be waking up

soon and he sent me here with some food. You must be hungry, you must, for you had naught to eat last night, and the miss, she said that you had had no luncheon, either. So I just brought a few things along at the master's direction."

While she spoke she placed the tray on the table next to his bed, shook out a linen cloth, and tucked it under his chin. In a moment she was ladling soup into his mouth with a spoon.

"There, there, young master, eat up. Don't talk so soon. It'll do no good."

As the soup reached his stomach, he realized how hungry he had been, and accepted her advice without demur.

She soon decided that his body was accepting the soup and turned to another plate on the tray. The bread from it was crumbled into the broth.

"There, now, this will do for a start, and a better start than any of us had hoped for this night past, for you were in a bad way, that's the reet of it, when they brought you into the manor."

After a while she stopped feeding him and sat back to observe the results of her efforts. "Your color's reet healthy now, excepting the black peeking out of those bandages. It's a lucky thing that t' other chap, he didn't hit you much harder, or you would have no been able to open up your mouth, not even for soup, eh?"

"He hit me plenty hard enough."

"Oh, aye. That be reet. But we do hear you put up a bonny fight of it, eh, lad?"

"Not bonny enough, it would seem."

"Ah, aye, there be time enough for that, time enough." She began to gather up her tray and utensils, her mission completed, with a burst of her earlier speed.

"Wait a moment, please, don't leave me now," Kit begged.

"Not leave now? With the butter to churn you'd have me sit and visit?"

"Please just answer a question or two."

"Oh, aye."

Taking this to mean encouragement of a sort, Kit blurted out his uppermost worry. "Miss Kitty Leyburne, the young lady who was with me. Is she all right? Where is she?"

"She be fine and fit, she be. She and Ole Master are down t' kennels, or so I judge from the sound of all those good-for-nothin' dogs howling yon."

"The master? Who is the master? To whom am I indebted for all this kindness?"

"Why, he be Ole Master. All folk hereabout know him."

"But I'm not from this District."

"Aye, that be plain enough." She had returned everything, including the linen chincloth, to the tray and had it between her two sturdy hands. "He be the one who inherited the land and title, not that he always use 'em the way he ought. Not he."

"Yes, but what is his name? What is the name of this place?"

She turned to him with brown eyes like saucers. "Well, surely, young master, you ought to be knowing Ole Master! You being so much alike even old Jock did wonder." She shook her head and grinned down at him. "And you say you know non about it? Why lad, you've come home! This is

Helm Pele and it and all about it will be yours some day. Ole Master, he be Sir Matthew de Fleming, one that some folk call a lord and all. Your uncle."

Twenty-two

The last party of searchers quitted their task only when all of their torches had failed them. They had been disheartened by their lack of success, frustrated by the darkness that had contributed to their failure, and unwilling to face their employer with their sad tidings. Miss Kitty was universally liked, for there had never been a kindlier nor friendlier young lady about and each of the men cherished the conviction that he was on a special footing with her. One had led her out on her pony when she was a tot, another had shown her how to nurse a sickly hoggett, a third had seen her nearly every day of her life. The youngest recalled the time he and she had climbed that old apple tree in the far field and found themselves unable to climb down, not an unhappy fate with all that fruit to dispose of. That Mr. Leyburne and his good lady would be distressed with their lack of news went without saying. It was to be expected. But every cottage and hut in the area, no matter how humble, would feel much the same grief.

It was their honor to encounter the young messenger from Helm Pele and be the first to hear the glad tidings. The boy was surprised to find himself carried on the shoulders of two burly men all the way up the drive to the portico of the Hall, there to find the master of the house waiting for him, warned of his news by a searcher sent on ahead at a trot.

All was well. Miss Kitty, and the youngster she seemed to dote on, were in the care of a near neighbor, having survived some adventure without serious harm befalling either. True, the lad had gotten his eye blackened along the way, they had been lost in the fog and thought themselves in fearful danger for a while, and a meal or two had been missed, but they were alive and safe.

With such a cause for rejoicing, Mr. Leyburne generously ordered a keg of ale to be broached and invited his employees and neighbors to join him in a toast of celebration. With such a reason to be thankful, the party was a merry one, and everyone departed for bed with feelings of ease and relief.

Well, almost everyone . . .

"They must be rescued from that pirate at once!" Mrs. de Fleming protested vehemently as she served herself from a plate of ham on the ladened sideboard in the breakfast parlor.

"Poor, dear Kitty must be saved from the clutches

of those men!" Mrs. Brampton trumpeted through mouthfuls.

"From that renegade!"

"From the two of them! Imagine, having such a ruffian, such a scandalous figure, for a relative!"

"From the two . . . ! Do you dare imply that that chit of a girl stands in any danger from my son, who so courageously rescued her from her own folly but yesterday?" She was unable to close her mouth, she was so dismayed by the insult she had just heard.

"A notorious character, your uncle! I'm not without some experience in the world, madam, and I well know that tendencies of *that* sort run in a family. How you could have the audacity to hoodwink us regarding your nearest connection, I shall never comprehend."

"Hoodwink? It was you who was pleased enough that my nearest connection, as you so mistakenly call that terrible man, was a nobleman of title and wealth with no other heir than my poor, dear son."

"I shall go today to fetch Kitty home, ladies," Mr. Leyburne said as if nothing had gone before. His wife, her hand trembling, handed him a cup of tea.

"One man alone would not be able to rescue her!" Mrs. Brampton protested. "Send for the militia! The Pele must be stormed by force!"

"You would fetch only your daughter? What of my son?"

"If he is well enough to travel he is welcome to accompany us back here to the Hall."

"Send for a litter! My poor baby must be rescued at all costs, no matter what his state!"

"Rescue? Rescue that young scoundrel? Leave him there to rot, I say!"

"Rot? How dare you, you, you . . . !"

"An armed escort at the very least, Leyburne. You must not face this danger alone. You must get her back to her mother's care as quickly as possible, and force may be the only argument that villain will heed."

"When my aunt, Lady Wilberham, hears of this insult you've made me, you shrew, she will see that you are barred forever from polite . . ."

Mr. Leyburne cleared his throat.

"I had thought to spend the night at the Pele."

This calm statement drew a sudden silence, one heavy with shock and disapproval. Naturally it was Mrs. Brampton who first asserted herself to see if she had heard him aright.

"Spend the night in that den of thieves? I cannot have but mistaken what you said. Spend the night? It is unimaginable!"

"Unimaginable?" He reached a lazy hand toward the rack of toast, ignoring his wife's pleading expression without a qualm. "I have done so before. It is quite a comfortable place."

"Visited Helm Pele? You are on such terms with him?"

"Never heard of such a thing!"

"The man is notorious!"

"A villain!"

"Shocking!"

The two ladies had finally found grounds for agreement and proceeded to support one another in this vein for some minutes. Mr. Leyburne remained unruffled by it all, a circumstance that only served to incense them the more.

"I shall not have my precious boy associated with such a family as this!" Mrs. de Fleming cried with spirit, her muffin forgotten. "Friends of outlaws! Nay, associates! I will forbid the banns!"

"Well, Kit may have something to say about that," he answered with a sardonic grin.

"Kit will do as his mama directs him, or else . . ." She said this last with conscious menace, but was disappointed with the response it drew from the others.

"Well? What else?" she was calmly asked.

"I shall cut off his allowance, that is what I shall do! He will be penniless!"

"Until his twenty-first birthday, in any case. Then I venture he will come into what little his father left him," Leyburne agreed.

This was yet another cause for anger. "How dare you imply that my dear late husband did not leave his son amply provided for!" the outraged widow and mother stormed.

"Well, he didn't, and that's a fact!" Mrs. Brampton suddenly snorted. "It was my money that was to sweeten this match, was it not? That has been fully understood from the start."

"It has been understood in some quarters, I grant you," Mr. Leyburne agreed amiably, turning an interested eye in her direction.

"W-e-ell!" She drew out this simple word with a tone that invested it with all the meanings in a dictionary, giving her audience a full opportunity to savor the look of forboding she had used. Their hostess was near tears, but unable to murmur a word in the face of her husband's strictures of silence.

"Well," Mr. Leyburne replied.

"Well! I am not at all sure that I wish to continue such a close association with a family of such scandalous connections and repute. First you encourage the attentions of a gazetted fortune hunter who has proven most unsatisfactory!"

The truce was over. "It was that wretched girl's fault!" Mrs. de Fleming cried out.

"You have allowed him to destroy your daughter's reputation, first by traipsing about the countryside alone together, so that her good name cannot help but be tarnished."

"My Kit!"

Nothing would stop the other woman. "To top off this folly, we now know that the two of them spent the night together. . . ."

"How dare you imply such conduct!" This from Mrs. de Fleming again.

"With only the presence of a known criminal, a scandalous figure notorious throughout the countryside, to lend her countenance. We can well imagine what took place, what debauchery the child endured. *And* now you would tell me that this dreadful man is someone you have accepted into the neighborhood with more than mere civility! You have become positively boon companions of his! I cannot bring myself to contemplate," (although here it was plain from the look in her eyes that this was just what she was so enjoying) "the scenes of depravity which have taken place in that den, with your full knowledge and contrivance if not your actual participation. . . ."

"Stop this instant!"

To the amazement of everyone, and her husband's particular pleasure, Mrs. Leyburne, her meekness set aside, was now on her feet, eyes blazing, a butter spreader clasped in her hand.

"You are a wicked, evil old hag to say such a thing about my dear Kitty! She is a dear, sweet girl. And *I* have no reason to suspect Kit, or his uncle, capable of such conduct. As to your vile lies about my husband, I will have you know that not one word of them is true! They are but the sordid imaginings of a silly old woman."

"W-e-ell!" Mrs. Brampton said once again, after her shock had worn off. "I no longer wish to be associated with such riffraff!" she intoned with satisfaction.

"And we have no longer any desire to countenance the presence of a vulgar, ill-bred social climber such as you!" her hostess snapped back, the butterknife waving.

"Well! Such ingratitude! Well! I shall shake the dust of this place from my heels soon enough!"

"Does that mean you're leaving?" Mr. Leyburne asked with pleased interest.

Until that moment Mrs. Brampton had been enjoying to the fullest the drama of the scene, but this simple question brought her back to practicalities. Drama was all very well and good, after all, but to be cutting herself off from a well-connected family, perhaps even to be kicked out of their house, was too important a matter to be undertaken without due consideration. Her face must have reflected her quandary, for Leyburne gave her no chance to answer.

"Good. I shall have your carriage called out. Do you suppose your maid can have your things packed in an hour or so? Or would you rather we sent your baggage after you?"

He had the satisfaction of seeing her at a loss for words. He turned to Mrs. de Fleming next.

"Madam, you will naturally wish to linger long enough to hear word of your son's condition. I would be inhuman to require you to depart in such circumstances, despite the provocations you have showered on me and my family. You may remain until the precise state of Kit's health has been determined and he is able to indicate his own wishes."

"I shall not deign to remain here one moment longer!" she gasped.

"Where do you intend to go? To your uncle-in-law's? I misdoubt the welcome you will receive at the Pele."

She too sought refuge in stony silence.

"As I have already stated, Kit will always enjoy a welcome at Leyburne Hall."

His wife had come to be standing beside him, and he gently disengaged her fingers from the cutlery she still clung to. "Come, my dear, I think your duties as a hostess have at long last come to an end. And I must depart for the Pele if I am to arrive in good time. Good-day, ladies!"

With a formal bow to his guests, he led his wife from the room.

Twenty-three

A howling noise reached Kit's ears as he entered the great yard of the old house. Despite his worst fears, this was not what he had expected. As fast as his unsteady feet would carry him, he moved toward the area of the disturbance.

"Now, Miss Kitty, this youngster is Blackie's Ear," a strong, carrying voice was saying just around the corner of a shed. A pleased whining sound began from the same direction.

"Blackie's Ear? It looks to me that there is a whole dog here, and not just an ear, Lord Helm."

The cackle this sally drew caused the hairs on Kit's neck to rise, and he swayed around the wall of the shed in time to see that the old man with the beak nose was still grinning.

"His dam was Blackie, miss, as you can well

guess. It's these uncommon long ears of his that gave him his name. He likes you, d'you see it?"

It was hard not to notice the hound's regard for Kitty, for he had just placed two large, muddy paws on her dress and was busy licking her face with a very pink tongue that was almost as long as the ears.

"M'lord, I fear you should have named him Blackie's Tongue. Or Blackie's Paws."

Helm laughed again. "It's usually the ears that catch one's attention."

He was turned in the direction of the house, looking over Kitty's shoulder, so it was he who saw Kit's unsteady approach into the kennel yard. The dogs howled their welcome.

"Ah, we have company. Hail the young hero!" Despite the sting of the words, there was a hint of pride in the way the older man held out his hand to the younger. "My nephew, I presume?"

"Sir, my lord, you have the advantage of me!" was all poor Kit could manage to sputter while his hand was being shaken vigorously.

"Kit, you are awake!" Kitty cried as she spun around. She met him with both hands outspread and pulled him closer to the other man.

"And steadier on your pins, judging by the distance you have just covered. Where the h—, er, dash was that footman I set to watching you? He was supposed to call me when you was ready for a visit."

"Kit, you will never guess who has given us help!" Kitty added.

"I've been informed," the youth answered grimly.

The other two exchanged a glance, then ignored the tone of his voice.

"Such a coincidence to end up here, of all the places in the District." She was smiling her delight and Kit suspected that it was inspired more by his ability to walk down a flight of stairs and across the lawn than by pleasure in his kinsman's company.

Then she added, "To meet a relative, and such a close one for the first time, and in circumstances that can only rouse gratitude and admiration is a remarkable thing, isn't it, Kit?" She ended this speech by prodding him in the ribs.

He stared at her, aghast. For some inexplicable reason, Kitty seemed to like his great-uncle. . . . No! Kit couldn't bring himself to acknowledge such a relationship with a notorious criminal. But Kitty had taken a liking for Lord Helm! It was past believing!

"I d' hear you did yourself proud against some cavalry ruffian yesterday, lad," his lordship said with a note of satisfaction in his voice, although his eyes lingered on the hounds. "Well done. Good to know you've some spunk in you, the last of the line and all. Your mama ain't turned you lily livered yet, not the way she did your father! Praise heaven for one small favor."

Blackie, mother of Ear, came forward and demanded her master's attention, so that Kit was able to direct a horrified stare at Kitty, trying to communicate some of the pent-up feelings in his bosom.

"It's all right," she hissed.

"What?"

"He is really quite nice. Not at all what we expected."

Kit directed a horrified glance at the bent shoulders of the other man. It was a blessing that their host's attention was taken up with the bitch for an unaccountably long time.

"How can you . . . ?"

"Do be calm . . . !"

"We are in the gravest danger!"

"Not at all. Trust me!"

"He is a pirate!"

"Yes, but . . ."

"The worst sort of cutthroat!"

"No!"

"Kitty!"

"It was only . . ."

Their host had regained his feet, and Kit found his next words choke off as he stared up into the piercing eyes of the taller man. If he had been more composed, he would have noticed a twinkle there, and better heeded Kitty's words.

"So as Miss Kitty was explaining a minute before, what happened yesterday is all for the best. Now, we don't stand on any parlor-room niceties here," at this point Kit found his shoulders clutched in the bony arm of his relative, "you're to get your health back, and then we shall get better acquainted and you shall begin learning the . . ."

"Sir, it is impossible that I linger here. It is my duty to return Miss Leyburne to her family, immediately! They are unaware of her whereabouts and will naturally be frantic with . . ."

"I sent a boy over to the Hall last night, so don't

you worry about that. Shame you got a bruise or two, but neither of you came to serious harm, and the adventure's brought us together in a way we ordinarily couldn't have done, not with that interfering mother of yours poking her nose into everything!"

"Sir! I will thank you not to speak of my mother in such terms!"

"Why not? I always have and I always will, and to her face when the opportunity's there. Is she as foolish as she once was, and meddling? And bossy?" The arm around Kit's shoulders squeezed them like an accordian.

Despite this handicap, Kit made an effort to gain control of the situation. "Just what is this all about?" he asked in his most austere voice, ignoring the pleading look on Kitty's face.

"This?" Lord Helm glanced around. "Miss Kitty and I are planning a hunt."

"That is not what . . ."

"A fox hunt, Kit," Kitty explained quickly.

"Not like those riding affairs they mount in the lowlands, either, lad, but a real fox hunt."

The swirl of voices carried away what little authority Kit might have had. "What are you talking about? That isn't what I . . ."

"In this District we must kill the foxes for the sake of the flocks."

"Foxes and *wolves*, too!" Kitty interjected.

"Well, not many of them any more, lass. In any case, there are plenty of foxes to bother us, and they're enough of a danger to the hoggetts."

"Hoggetts?"

"Lambs, Kit. And so all the landowners and

sheep herders in the District combine their hunting packs and track down the vermin," she explained, anxious to keep the talk in these less controversial channels.

"Precisely. And we do it on foot, for the land hereabout's too rough for galloping about. I had thought to send word over to Mr. Leyburne and see if he would care to join us, but now that he's coming . . ."

"Join? Coming? Do you mean he's on visiting terms with you?"

Helm ignored the interruption. "I had the lad I sent to the Hall ask Mr. Leyburne to ride over today, to inspect your injuries himself and be better able to reassure the ladies of Miss Kitty's well-being. He'll be here by teatime, if I have read his note correctly, and will stay the night."

Kit's look of dismay was replaced with one of confusion. "Mr. Leyburne will spend the night here?"

"Of course."

"Oh."

Mr. Leyburne? A sensible, well-respected man who was willing to accept the hospitality of the terrible Lord Scandal. Not a young, impressionable, naive girl like Kitty who had somehow been charmed, or was afraid, or . . . ?

Perhaps there was some sort of subterfuge here. Mr. Leyburne wasn't really coming. Or he was forced to make the visit, to rescue his daughter from such a danger. But if Kitty hadn't come to harm last night, where was the threat? Surely a pirate would have seized the opportunity when it first offered to do what he would to so innocent a girl. As Kit's mind swirled, he wondered if he had wandered between the covers of one of his mother's favorite novels.

Mr. Leyburne was a justice of the area. He could summon the full fury of the law against anyone who threatened his daughter. And this was civilized England, not the barbaric Caribbean. And Kitty, for all her youth, was not really very foolish, not at all. If she liked the old man too . . . ?

The bony embrace of his shoulders had begun to feel better than it had, for Kit found his knees growing weak in an embarrassing way. As if sensing this, Lord Helm led the way back to the lawn and the rustic seats that were standing near its edge.

"Let's sit a while, lad. We'll have time enough for everything. There's a lot of territory to cover. Years worth, in fact. I've been putting this place back into some sort of order, and I welcome the chance to show it off. I never thought to live to see the day when I could do it with you, my heir and one I can be proud of, and I don't intend to let you slip away! Tell me of this confrontation you had with the cavalry, eh?"

"What I did was little and poorly executed, m'lord! It is Kitty who showed the most amazing pluck and courage!" Somehow it was proving easier to talk to this intimidating stranger than he would ever have thought. "You should have seen her supporting me over the trod! And walking beside the pony!" He threw her a grateful look, the awkwardness of the present predicament forgotten.

She blushed and quickly answered, "No, not at all! Kit was magnificent! The way he stood up to that dreadful man and then kept walking even when his jaw was hurting him so!"

Now it was Kit's turn to blush, amazed at the warmth of Kitty's praise.

"It seems that between the two of you, you managed things quite well. I can't in all honesty say that I'm sorry it all happened, but there's no point going into all that. Foolish of me not to have made a push to meet you before this. You're my heir after all." For a moment a gruff frown settled between the deep-set eyes. A gleam of satisfaction replaced it.

"But we'll make up for all that now, won't we? The first thing is for you to get really back on your feet, not in this wobbly fashion you've been showing us today, and then we'll go into it more. Fair enough?"

Without waiting for a reply, he rose to his feet and bellowed, drawing a response from the house and barn. "I'll just have a couple of men give you an arm on the stairs, and you'll have a chance to rest before Mr. Leyburne comes. You might want to discuss this and that with him while he's here, eh?" He winked broadly at the young people, then gave the servants his orders.

Kit, bursting with questions, was helped into the house, betrayed by his own weakness and unable to satisfy his burning curiosity. The minute his head touched his pillow, he slept.

Twenty-four

To arrive at Helm Pele after the breakfast he had experienced in his own home was like stepping off the stage of a melodrama back into real life. Mr. Leyburne looked with satisfaction at the gardeners scything the grass of the lawn, the groom leading a horse toward a paddock, maidservants vigorously polishing the many panes of a tall window in the front of the house. It was a scene of ordered prosperity founded on hard work and sound management. Altogether more to his taste than the company of mesdames Brampton and de Fleming.

His satisfaction grew when he saw the happy smile on Kitty's face. So, the ladies' dire fears were unfounded. He would almost have tolerated their company for the satisfaction of watching them react to the atmosphere of common sense all around him. He feared that they would find sanity and measured reason little to their taste.

"You look well, Kitty!" he said with a private smile he saved only for her. "And Kit?"

"Kit is this minute waking from a nap. He has had the most awful time of it, Papa! He was so brave!"

"So I understood from the message I received. But no serious injury was done, I gather?"

"A black eye. And a sore jaw." She looked up at him with sudden anxiety. "Are they serious?"

"Only briefly, my love. Here is our host, we must greet him, then I wish to have some private talk with you. Hello, Helm."

There were some minutes of courteous exchanges before Mr. Leyburne was forced to tell his daughter of the change wrought in her fortune. Although he was sure that the departure of Mrs. Brampton from their lives was a good thing, and would not seriously affect the girl's happiness, he nonetheless knew that she might not be convinced of this, especially if her feelings for Kit were as he suspected them to be. With a sigh, he took up the burden of his tale after their host had left them to their *tête à tête,* knowing full well that he was the sole agent of Kitty's loss of luxurious prosperity.

Her inquiries after the other residents of the Hall provided him with an easy opening for his news.

"All are well, although I fear that Mrs. Brampton will not be there to greet your return."

"Not there? Was she called away on urgent business? Is there some crisis with Mr. Brampton?"

"No, the crisis was wholly at the Hall, my dear. I have unfortunate news to tell you."

It was inconceivable to Kitty that her godmother, always so doting and at times oversolicitous of her health, would have left the area before she had personally seen that Kitty was well.

"She simply left? She wasn't called away?" she asked with confusion.

"Yes, and I must own that it is mostly my fault that our family has incurred her displeasure." When he saw that she had nothing to say to that, he took a breath and went on with his tale.

"The news of your disappearance naturally aroused considerable alarm amongst us. There were many hours of anxious waiting while the search parties were sent out. The last could be heard returning soon after midnight, their torches burnt out, and for a moment we had lost all hope. Then the messenger from the Pele arrived, telling of your safe rescue there. He also recounted some of your adventures."

It was here that the story became difficult to tell, for he did not wish to dwell on the bitter arguments that had prevailed between Mrs. de Fleming and Mrs. Brampton during the wait for word of the couple. Even after they heard the good news, the ladies could not put aside their ill will. It would not do to let the girl know that two such ladies, with every reason to feel the darkest concern for the missing pair, had spent so many hours in feuding with one another, more concerned with their mutual animosity, rather than in worry and prayer for the missing children.

"We were naturally pleased that you were well,

but as you may not be aware of, Lord Helm is not held in good repute by his own family, Mrs. de Fleming in particular. She was upset that Kit, and you, should be sharing his home with him and relying on his generosity."

"And Mrs. Brampton?"

"I fear that Mrs. Brampton had formed a harsh opinion of Kit's character. She blamed him for the difficulties you two found yourselves in, even adding more trouble to the tale than had actually happened. Mrs. de Fleming, in her anxiety to defend Kit, blamed you, insisting that you had somehow led him into danger."

"I fear they were both right, in some sense. Kit took me to a glade, then wished to climb a chimney, and I wandered off to explore by myself while I awaited his return."

"Both innocent enough actions, but perhaps a trifle foolhardy. In any case, not blameworthy. However," and here he had to choose his words carefully, "the appearance of the thing was bad, and as the ladies argued, each in the defense of one of you, their language became stronger and the accusations more violent."

"Accusations?"

"When I let it be known that I had welcomed Helm as a neighbor, they both turned on me. Their accord didn't last very long, but they made it clear that I, and my family, were deeply suspect for exercising any familiarity with someone they both denounced as a pirate and a notorious criminal." He smiled wryly at the memory.

"How dare they! He is the nicest man imaginable! All he did was smuggle wad once, and have the bad luck to be caught. It was all but a lark!"

"The fact that his offense was minor seems to have been forgotten over the years."

"But I like him!"

He smiled again. "I fear that would carry little weight with the ladies."

"And they have no right dictating to you. You must choose your own friends!"

"I rather felt that way, too. In the heat of the moment, Mrs. Brampton carried her criticism beyond young Kit and declared that your reputation was ruined, mainly because your mother and I had permitted Kit to spend time with you, often alone."

"But it was she . . . !"

"Precisely. It was she and Mrs. de Fleming, another quick to blacken your name, who had first concocted the scheme, and over my express protests. She felt that yesterday's adventure was but a natural result of your friendship with Kit, and put the worst possible interpretation on your having spent the night together here at the Pele with only Lord Helm, whom she termed as a ruffian of the worst sort, to chaperone you."

Kitty's face was flaming now and her eyes snapped with anger. She was not the sort of sheltered miss who would mistake the other's meaning. "I trust you showed her the door!"

"Well, not quite!"

"But you said she had left!"

He cleared his throat with a dry cough and said modestly, "I contented myself with calling for her carriage."

"Good for you! That is exactly what you should have done, Papa! I'm so proud of you for standing up to her!"

He held up a warning hand. "Kitty, there is more. Perhaps if I had exercised more tact, this scene would never have taken place, at least I think your mother believed so at the time. But Mrs. Brampton's leaving has important consequences on your own fortune."

Kitty's face fell. "Oh, no. The dowry!"

"I fear you have discovered the effect of her anger all too well. She has announced that she will no longer consider you her protégée. She has withdrawn all her promises of providing you with a marriage portion, whether you marry Kit or another."

She had begun to cry and he looked at her somewhat helplessly as he tried to find a handkerchief in his pockets. This was even worse than he had expected! If she had been angry he could have borne that meekly enough; instead she was crushed.

"Then there will be no reason for my betrothal with Kit to be pursued! It was plain to me that he and his mother were interested in me for the money." She recalled Kit's worldly speech on the advantages of money all too well.

"That may have been the case in the beginning, darling, but I believe his feelings for you have been undergoing a change as he has come to know you."

She shook her head.

"How could they? He is in love with another. Truly in love, not just dreaming as I have done!"

He stared at her, thunderstruck. "How can you know about that?"

"I saw them together. Often. In the Park." She was gasping out her words between sobs, but her meaning was clear enough. "I saw how they looked at one another! I so envied them their happiness."

Mr. Leyburne had been well aware of the attachment between Kit and Lady Madge, and he had put that down to youthful folly. It happened all too often that a young man's first passion was for an older, more experienced woman, but usually little came of it. However, he had had no idea that Kitty had suspected the relationship.

He set himself grimly to put things to right. "I must stand by what I just said, Kitty. Kit's attachment to another woman did exist. Yes, I knew of it and it was one reason for wishing any formal announcement of the betrothal postponed. But I am sure that his feelings have changed. The lady is married, in any case."

Kitty's face cleared. That explained much that had been troubling her. "But . . . how can true love change?"

"My darling little ninny, who said it was true love? These things happen. And I have heard that Lady Madge has recently been seen about in the company of a certain merchant. I would guess that the relationship with Kit was broken off. It would have been the honorable thing for them to do in the circumstances."

"Broken off? But Papa, I would rather give up Kit than see him unhappy! If he loves Lady Madge, he should marry her! Somehow!"

Mr. Leyburne considered all he knew about

Lady Madge, but it was more than he could confide in so young a girl. "But does he love her?" he asked with a sigh. "Can you be so sure?"

"How can I be sure of anything?" By this time he had found his handkerchief and she was sobbing into it.

After a moment of thought, he offered the only solution he knew of. "Then we must test Kit."

"Test him?"

"Yes. We shall provide him with an honorable excuse for withdrawing from the engagement."

"Couldn't we just ask him what his feelings are?"

"We can hardly expect him to confess to duplicity in this matter, Kitty. If it is as you say and he loved Lady Madge, he could not wish to announce this. And as a gentleman he would feel bound to protest his regard for you. But I think we can test him on two counts, not just one. If he passes both, then will you believe me?"

"I could not bear to watch him turn away from me! I would rather never know!"

"But if he doesn't turn away, will you have him?"

"Yes, but you must do it all."

"Now, that would hardly be fair. It is in some small way your concern, too." A sudden smile lit his face, one of exasperated humor. "However, as I said, there are two tests. How would you like for me to apply the first one, then if all goes well, send him on to you?" he suggested.

"Well, yes, I could face him if I didn't feel so absolutely sure that he would reject me," she agreed after a pause. "I can tell him I have no dowry. But what is this other test? Can there be two reasons for him to withdraw honorably from our engagement?"

"Yes, there are two. It's amazing anyone gets married at all, don't you think? There are so many good arguments against it." He hesitated over telling her of Mrs. de Fleming's opposition, then decided it would have more meaning for her coming from Kit's own mouth. To hear him declare that he was willing to withstand his mama for her sake would be the best tonic in the world for Kitty's spirits. She had had too poor an opinion of herself for too long.

"Don't bother me with questions now, Kitty. You shall know soon enough. I have much to see to before tea, and your mama packed something for you to change into. Run along and make yourself pretty and leave the rest to me."

Twenty-five

When Mr. Leyburne had finally completed his program of intrigue, the hour for tea had arrived and the house party perforce had gathered to enjoy this meal. The tradition was such that it was unthinkable not to do so, despite all that had happened.

Of the four people there, only Mr. Leyburne could be said to actually be enjoying himself. For that matter, he was the only one the least bit comfortable. All was going to plan and he was well satisfied. Any doubts that were in order would have to wait for later.

It was a scrumptious meal. Plum cake, shortbread, crumpets and muffins, thin bread spread with butter, tiny sandwiches, sweet biscuits, all washed down with the tea. The meal was served under the trees. Kitty poured, Blackie's Ear made an appearance and was shooed away, but only after he had successfully begged some chicken from the sandwiches. The adventure of the previous day might have been centuries old, and the anxious news that Mr. Leyburne had imparted was not once referred to.

Yet the atmosphere was glum.

Kit had welcomed a private interview with Mr. Leyburne, surprised and flattered that the other had sought it, and determined to make the best of his opportunity. There were many things on his mind that he wished to share with the older man, not the least of which was the precise status of his uncle, Lord Helm, with whom he could *not* feel at ease. But before he could press Mr. Leyburne for permission to set a date with Kitty for the wedding, the older man had sadly told him of Mrs. de Fleming's opposition to any such match, in fact, that she had insisted that Kit heed her command to break off the engagement.

Stunned, Kit said not a word against his mother, for what could be said? The news that she would cut off his allowance if he dared oppose her will seemed to stiffen his resolve, and with apologies and explanations to make seemly his unfilial actions to Mr. Leyburne, he pressed for Kitty's hand in marriage.

"For you see, sir, I do care for her awfully, and even if we can't tie the knot now, I'll have a bit of income when I'm of age. If there's to be no other blunt for us right away, I'd like to plan on marrying her then, if she agrees and you agree."

"I can appreciate that if you are in love with my daughter, you must make your own decision in the matter, although I should naturally prefer your mother's approval."

"Well, I daresay she'll come around," he protested vaguely.

"And if she does not, two years is a long time to wait," Mr. Leyburne said with mendacious doubt.

"Yes, well, I shall quite understand if Kitty says no. Or at least says to wait on the engagement. She's young and it wouldn't be fair to bind her when she might be finding someone else to love. Perhaps I ought not to say anything to her after all. . . ."

"No, no, let her decide for herself, young man!" the other said quickly, seeing that once again self-denial, nobly and lovingly intended, was going to ruin all his plans.

So Kit endured the meal in unhappy silence, the difficulties concerning his uncle's reputation put aside. He spent most of his time casting looks at his fellow sufferer, unaware of what she was feeling and afraid to catch her eye, for his might prove all too eloquent. While he fumbled with cup and plate, sugar and cream, he also fumbled in his mind for the right words to say when at last he had his promised meeting with her.

And how was Lord Helm during all this? Why couldn't he feel the part of genial host he was trying halfheartedly to uphold? He did manage to discuss crops with Mr. Leyburne, for in all decency they must cover the damned awkward silence of the youngsters. And there was the fox hunt to go into—that held some of his attention. But it was hard not to interfere, a thing he was itching to do. He would set them all right! Why shouldn't he? He was the head of the family, after all, and had a say in the matter. So between bites of macaroons and barked comments about this and that, glum and dissatisfied, he worried the situation like a dog with a bone. But as Leyburne had insisted, and as Leyburne knew the youngsters better than he, he supposed he ought to listen to the feller's advice.

And Kitty fiddled with the hot tea, unaware of Kit's worried glances, trying in every way she knew how to hide her own discomfort and succeeding only in hiding her face.

Blackie's Ear escaped the kennel once again and wandered back to the tea party, eager for more refreshments.

"Take that cur away, damn him!" Lord Helm cried with exasperation. "You two youngsters, drag him back to the kennel! He fair dotes on you, Miss Kitty, he'll follow you anywhere. Kit, you go along and help her out. And be sure he's tied up good and proper this time." He sat back with one more slice of cake, ignoring their compliance with his commands.

Kit leaped to his feet with alacrity, a nod from Mr. Leyburne assuring him of that gentleman's acquiescence, and with a lunge laid his hand on the gnawed-off end of Ear's rope. Kitty followed more slowly, suffering the dog to lick her hands, glad it gave her an excuse to keep her eyes downcast. She too cast a stealthy glance in her father's direction, and was rewarded with a reassuring smile. Taking heart, she led the way to the kennels.

Twenty-six

Kit had some vague notion that he should go down on his knees to propose to Kitty. It was done so in all the novels he had ever read, and that was the best guide he had. After all, people didn't propose with an audience about, so he had never seen it done before.

But then in all the novels the important and interesting scene was set in a drawing room or parlor or in a nice, tidy garden. No one had ever proposed in a kennel yard, he was sure. It was altogether too muddy and smelly to kneel down here!

He was muttering to himself under his breath, trying to find the proper words, the elegant turn of phrase, wondering if an apology would perhaps be suitable to explain his lack of correct form. Or he could lure her out to the garden. That was it! But wait, the gentlemen were there.

Blackie's Ear was gnawing through the new rope.

"Yes?" Kitty asked.

"What?"

"Didn't you say something? I thought I heard you say something."

"Oh! It's nothing much, or rather, it's important, I suppose, it's just that . . ."

"Yes?"

He nodded several times with satisfaction. "There was this dream I wanted to tell you about! Yes, that's it!"

Kitty swallowed her disappointment. "A dream? The waking sort or the kind you have when you sleep?"

"Not a daydream, you know, but sort of a mild nightmare." Now that he was launched, words flowed in a torrent. "It was about yesterday, and I was with a lady in blue, only I couldn't see her face. You know how it is in dreams? We did all sorts of things together and I still couldn't see her face, it was as if she wouldn't let me. Anyway, I guessed it was someone I used to know in London, judging by the way she acted," here he had the grace to blush, "and I was disappointed because there was something I had to tell her, only for some reason I didn't want to, and then I found out it was you and everything was all right!"

Kitty looked at him with some perplexity. "It made everything right to find it was me who was with you?"

"Yes, of course! I had to tell her I loved her and I

didn't, not at all, so when she turned into you everything worked out, so to speak! You see, I could tell *you* what it was all about. It seemed the easiest thing in the world when I was dreaming, all I had to do was pop the question. It's dashed more complicated now, but I'd rather it was you, because, well, because of being . . . What I mean to say, I'm fond of you."

Kitty no longer looked perplexed, only angry, but Kit failed to notice this.

"I'm more than fond of you!" he suddenly blurted.

"Oh, Kit!"

"I don't care if my mama doesn't like the match, I won't let her come between us!"

Now understanding was superseding all her other emotions and Kitty smiled up at Kit. "You mean you would defy your mama for me?"

"Dash it all, yes, I would. And I don't care if it seems disloyal or whatever, it's just that a feller has to take charge of his life, don't you know?"

"Yes, I know! I'm so proud of you!" Another heavy silence fell and he still hadn't said the magic words. "Does this mean we shall always be friends?"

"Of course! That goes without saying!"

"Oh, just friends."

He looked at her with surprise. Then once again the words were coming fast and he said what he had to in a jumble. "More than that! I love you, Kitty! I was going to propose to you in better form than this, I'm sorry I can't bring myself to kneel when I ask you to marry me, but this yard is full of muck and it would ruin my trousers and they're the only pair I've got at the moment, and I didn't think you'd mind, you being such a sensible girl and all. You don't, do you? Mind that I'm not on my knees?"

"No, and yes."

"What?" He looked crushed.

"No, I don't mind that you aren't down on your knees. Not at all. And yes, I shall be very pleased to marry you. I do so love you!"

"You do? You're not just saying that? Dash it all, that's fine, demn fine! You've made me the happiest feller in the world, Kitty!" He flailed about with his arms, finally taking one of her hands in both of his, as if he didn't quite know what to do with it. "I want to live in this District, does that suit you?" He paused long enough to see her nod her head yes, then continued, "And we will have to do without my allowance from my mama, but with what Mrs. Brampton's promised you one day, we'll manage just fine. In two years I'll come into my own money in any case, so we won't have to pinch pennies for long."

He turned back to her with a smile and was shocked by the expression on her face. "Kitty, love, what's wrong?" He seized her other hand, then, more daringly, put an arm around her shoulder.

"Oh, Kit!" was all she could say for some minutes, and he stood by her murmuring soothing words into her hair.

"It is so awful!" She realized now that the first test her father had devised for Kit was to face his mother's opposition to the match. Had he realized that this would mean the loss of Kit's slight income? Surely not! This was too harsh a test for anyone to bear!

"What is it, love? Just tell me and we shall fix it up between us. Don't worry, don't worry."

"But we can't 'fix' it! Mrs. Brampton has left the Hall!"

"Jolly good show, I say. What's so bad about that?"

She wrung her hands for a moment, her face turned to the ground, then she forced herself to face him. "She's cut me off!"

"Oh, Lord!"

"She said some horrible things about you and me and my father made her leave. He could do nothing else, Kit!"

"I'm sure of that," he answered stoutly. "But where does this leave us?"

They looked at each other doubtfully, then Kit made the first suggestion. "We could wait for two years, I suppose. There should be enough for us from what my father left, if we're careful."

Kitty's face lit up. "We could ask your uncle, Kit! You're the heir to the title, after all. It is only proper that you receive some sort of allowance from him."

He scowled at this suggestion, dashing her hopes. "I cannot accept a penny from him, Kitty! Do you have any idea of how he earned it? You know, we talked all about it. Piracy and stealing, and horrible things like murder and bloodshed are the foundation for his fortune. I just couldn't bring myself to accept his assistance, heir or no. I may even refuse his money if he leaves it to me!"

"But Kit, we were all wrong about that!"

"Kitty, love, I wish we were, but there can be no mistake. The facts are too well known."

"Do you suppose my father would sit there calmly drinking tea with him if that were true?"

"But . . . !"

"There are pirates and there are pirates! He wasn't really one at all, although it's the name the smugglers go by in these parts."

"What are you talking about? This makes no sense."

"He was caught smuggling wad! Plumbago! Not merchant ships in the West Indies!"

"Wad? Not pieces of eight?"

"No, it was all a silly lark in the first place. He did break the law, and the authorities found him out, and what he had done just happened to be something people around here call piracy, and that's how this mess all started."

"But he made a fortune in the West Indies!"

"Yes, his family helped him escape—they didn't want the scandal of a trial, and they shipped him off to the West Indies. And he became a merchant and a planter and made his money honestly!"

"How do you know all this?" Kit asked doubtfully.

"He told me so!"

"Dash it all, you can't take his word for it! Of course he'd say something like that!"

"It isn't just his word! My Papa and other respectable gentlemen in the district believe him!"

Suddenly they had drawn battle lines and Kit found himself facing a very angry young lady.

"Even if that is all true," he said in a quiet voice, "after the way we have treated him, Mama and I, do you think I could go and ask for an allowance, just like that? He has every reason to hate me!"

"He might dislike your *mama*. It is in large part her fault that things are so confused. But he must realize that you aren't to blame. How could you know the truth of something that happened so many years ago?"

"Even if he doesn't dislike me, he has no reason to treat me with kindness. Look at the way I've behaved toward him since we met! He must turn away from me in disgust."

"He would never be such a ninny! I believe he told me all he did in the hopes that you would finally know the truth."

"Kitty, darling, I couldn't beg from him, I couldn't! It would be dishonorable! I never should have asked you to marry me, not when I wasn't sure of my own situation. If you want to reconsider, I beg of you to do so. All that I can offer you is a long engagement and an impecunious marriage to end it. You can't possibly want that. I'd rather give you up than see you unhappy!"

And Kitty was suddenly sure. "We love one another and that's what counts. Now it is my turn to tell you that it will all work out. I'm sure of it! And I don't mind waiting, nor do I mind an impecunious match!"

Then they were in each other's arms clinging desperately.

Twenty-seven

Blackie's Ear provided the solution to Kit and Kitty's dilemma. Or rather, he led the solution to them, for once again, he had escaped the kennel.

When Lord Helm, who had long ago finished the tea in his cup and his macaroons, crumpets, biscuits, plum cake, bread and butter, sandwiches, in fact, everything left on the tea table after the couple's departure, saw the dog loose, he lost his temper.

"Now, what can those two young people be doing all this time? They certainly haven't tied up that demmed dog!" With a heavy lunge he got to his feet and stalked toward the kennel, not caring or noticing what Mr. Leyburne chose to do. With a shrug, his guest followed. So did the dog.

When Mr. Leyburne caught up with Helm, the old man was standing at the entrance to the yard, hands on hips, laughing softly. Kit and Kitty had yet to notice them.

"Well, it's about time you made up your minds. Although it was as plain as the nose on my face to me from the moment I saw you two together!" This assertion was undoubtedly truer than a similar one made by Mrs. de Fleming on an earlier occasion.

Now the lovers heard him. They sprang apart.

"Sir, Uncle, sir!"–Kit sputtered. Then he saw Mr. Leyburne. "Sir, Kitty and I have decided to become engaged," he explained to the girl's father, "even though we shall have to postpone the wedding. That is, if you don't mind? Sir?"

"Not at all."

"Postpone the wedding?" Helm roared. "Why in blazes do you want to do that?"

Blackie's Ear, startled by the loud voice, stopped scratching his shoulder and took notice.

"We don't want to, it's just that there doesn't seem to be any money for us to live on!"

"They could always move into the Hall with my wife and me," Mr. Leyburne murmured, apparently to the dog.

"Move into the Hall? No money? Have you all gone daft? Of course there's money!"

"Lord Helm, thank . . ." Kitty began.

Kit shushed her. "No, you shall let me handle this!" he commanded. To Mr. Leyburne's immense amusement, she did.

"I have been told by Mr. Leyburne that my mother disapproves of the match. While it grieves me to act contrary to her wishes, I feel I must do what I think right and proper, and, well, I love

Kitty too much not to marry her! But now of course Mama won't wish to continue my allowance, which is only natural after I have defied her, and it wouldn't have been enough by itself anyway, so we shall have to wait until I have control of my own money."

"Your own money? That wouldn't be enough to put a roof over your heads, you silly young fools!"

Kit blanched, then swallowed hard. "Then we shall just have to wait until . . ."

"The Hall it is," Mr. Leyburne told the sky.

"Wait until what?" The old man was very angry now. "My heir living on someone else's generosity, even that of his wife's family? Living hand to mouth? Have I wandered into Bedlam that I should hear such wild talk from you? You shall rely on me for an allowance. Of course!"

"Oh, thank you, sir!" Kitty said very quickly.

"But . . . !"

"It is the right and proper thing to do," Mr. Leyburne said as he ruthlessly cut off Kit's protest.

"I could not beg . . . !"

"Of course it's the thing to do! And there's that by-election over in my borough and you're to stand for it. And there's the town house to be opened up after all these years, and refurbished. That will be up to you, Kitty. And you must spend some time here at the Pele, to learn your way about, so to speak." The hound barked his approval.

Kitty took Kit's limp arm and began to tug him toward Lord Helm. "That sounds so wonderful! Thank you so much!" Poor Kit looked bewildered and speechless.

"You're to have a free hand with the London

place, Kitty, don't cheese pare! It must all be of the finest!"

"I have been in London so little, are you sure you wish to entrust this to me? I don't know that I could deal with it as it ought to be done."

"Never mind, if you don't like it, redo it."

Mr. Leyburne patted Kitty's free arm. "Your mother will be so pleased that it is all settled now. And I think Mrs. de Fleming will feel the same way in a few days."

Kit looked immensely relieved, and his expression became more cheerful.

"Who cares?" Lord Helm snapped. "I wish I could give you the Scandale title, Kit, but you ain't my son, so it won't do. Might be better in any case to let it rest awhile. By the time you have a son of your own to take it on, people will have forgotten some of my escapades!"

Kit turned to him, a solemn look on his face, finally with something to say. "Forget your escapades? Perhaps. But I shan't ever let a son of mine forget your kindness. You didn't have to offer me so much, I'd done nothing to deserve it!"

The old man turned a dark red, then barked, "We ought to leave these two to themselves, eh, Leyburne? Young love and all that. What do you say we try a hand of cards?"

Kit and Kitty could hear them discussing this all the way to the house, but they paid little attention to the words. They had so little need for talk themselves. Arm in arm, with Blackie's Ear padding beside Kitty, they turned to the garden in companionable silence.